THE BRIGHT PRISON

Also by Penelope Mortimer

A VILLA IN SUMMER

PENELOPE MORTIMER

THE BRIGHT PRISON

London
MICHAEL JOSEPH

First published by
MICHAEL JOSEPH LTD
26 Bloomsbury Street
London W.C.1
1956

Made and printed in Great Britain by Purnell
& Sons, Ltd. Paulton (Somerset) and London,
and set in Bembo Type, 12 point, leaded

For
JOHN

CHAPTER 1

At half-past three the long winter night, like an Arctic season, had already begun. The lamps were not yet lit in the streets but some cars had their sidelights on, and ground-floor rooms, as it was not time to draw the curtains, shone brilliantly, bursting into life with the click of a switch. There was, in this early darkness, a sense of danger. Traffic seemed to move faster; buses doubled their size, rocking, a blaze of light past request stops; cars looked evil, their orange indicators pointing this way and that, their drivers hunched desperate at the wheels; delivery vans, normally part of the placid day, drew up suddenly outside gaunt black houses, and boxes of grocery, baskets of laundry were thrown anyhow down basement steps; the postman delivered, savagely, letters to the wrong address.

But in the wide, dilapidated London street where the Paintons lived the sense of danger was remote. There was little traffic, only an underground steam railway which occasionally screamed through holes in the ground and shook the windows; where it went, where it came from, nobody knew. Except for the Paintons', none of the houses was lit. The rest were divided and subdivided and the subdivisions partitioned into bed-sitting-rooms for respectable, reasonably well-to-do professional people, people who did not often come home until it was time to go to bed, but joined little clubs or went to concerts or discussion groups or poetry readings, and at the weekends visited their parents or their married sisters, every spare moment obsessed with the problem of how not to return to Sheldon Road until they were too tired to care. Their landladies, army officers' widows with blue hair and formidable tweed suits, lived always at the back and watched their television sets unobserved, saving and saving money against the day when the leases would run out and they would have, somehow, to do ninety-nine years' work of repairs on the crumbling plaster, the mouldering stone. From these back rooms now, at half-past three, began the chorus of whistling kettles, all up and down the road, kettles screaming as though with some primitive urge from basement to basement.

Antonia Painton hurried down the stairs into the kitchen, turned down the gas and pulled the whistle off the kettle's snout; from next door the high whine continued unabated. She stood for a moment in the kitchen, with its cold white of refrigerator and washing machine, the cold white electric-light bulb reflected in the uncurtained window, and tugged desperately at the zip fastener on her dress. At the same time she looked at the three trays piled high with food and checked it all in her mind: sandwiches—tomato and honey and, sickeningly, chocolate spread; cakes, biscuits, meringues; orange-peel baskets precariously heaped with jelly; ice-cream, to be brought out at the last moment; and, last, the birthday cake. She straightened a candle, blew what looked like a speck of dust off the hard, crustated surface. It was a pretty cake, but none of them would eat it. For days it would appear at teatime, looking greyer, the icing fallen away like plaster off the walls of a derelict house; they would try it on the cat, crumbling it into enamel plates which they would leave about indefinitely in dark corners; in the end it would go in the dustbin. She twisted round, trying, impossibly, to see what was wrong with the zip fastener, gave it a last furious tug and caught the bare flesh underneath.

'What's the matter?' Georgina asked. She leant indolently against the kitchen door, her hands in the pockets of a pair of grotesque grey-flannel trousers which, from the bulge underneath her sweater, obviously reached up to her armpits; they were belted, tightly, with a luggage strap.

'What on earth have you got on?' Antonia asked. 'What on *earth*?'

'I found them.'

'Where did you find them?' But directly she had said it, she knew it didn't matter. 'Go and take them off. They'll be arriving in a minute. Honestly, Georgina——'

'Well. Why shouldn't I? They're all right, aren't they?'

Antonia looked at her. Georgina was twelve, thin, flat, always somewhere smudged with ink; at the

9

moment, like a cast mark, there was a blue smear in the middle of her forehead. In her clear, hard eyes, square hands, bony little hips there was nothing to indicate that she might some day change into a woman.

'They are not,' she said patiently, 'all right. They're ghastly. Didn't you look at yourself in the mirror?'

'Yes. I won't wear that soppy frock.'

Antonia turned, opened the door of the refrigerator, looked at the ice-cream. She said, her voice muffled, 'I told you to take them off. Put on what frock you like.'

'Why should I?' Georgina asked again, relentlessly.

'Because it's Charlotte's birthday party and you've got to be polite and you've got to—grow up!' Antonia finished explosively. She was angry because she felt helpless. 'What about Edward and Felicity—are they dressed? Oh, I'd better come up and see.' She took Georgina's shoulders, turned her round and guided her through the door. 'You're twelve,' she said; 'it's old.'

'Not as old as Daniel.'

'No, but you're a girl.' She didn't really know what she meant, and neither did Georgina. It so often happened that there was an idea, a feeling, a vague indication of some important or trivial truth and there was never time to sit down and find the right words for it, produce it neatly, intelligibly, as a fact of life. Her children, Antonia felt as she propelled Georgina up the dark stairs, depended for most of their information on sudden, mysterious statements which, without any context, became as impressive and meaningless as proverbs. A stitch in time saves nine; it's always darkest before dawn; you're old because you're a girl —it wasn't, she sympathised with Georgina, satisfactory.

The stairs, the landings of the tall house were like the street outside—cold, dark and catching the chest with fog; the open bedroom doors giving blasts of light and warmth on to the clammy linoleum, the cavernous hall, which, in their first enthusiasm on moving into the house, they had distempered a dour and forbidding red. Antonia shivered and longed, but only momentarily, for reprieve from the next unavoidable hours.

The three children were in the bedroom which was shared by Georgina and Charlotte. Antonia closed the door and said automatically, 'I told you to keep the door shut,' then stood for a moment like a general contemplating with apparent calm the best method of attack. Charlotte, of course, was ready. Blonde, smooth, beautiful, her feet crossed, her hands in her lap, her lashes lowered, she sat like a Victorian oleograph on her bed, her white net dress arranged carefully, a clean handkerchief, Antonia felt sure, in her knicker pocket. As Georgina came in and stood defiantly hitching her trousers Charlotte raised her eyes for a moment and said, with loathing, ' Beast.'

'Why?'

'You know why.'

'I don't!'

'You do!'

'Why then?'

'What you wrote in your diary.' She turned her unmoved, perfect face to Antonia. 'You do look nice. Shall I answer the door when they come?'

'Yes. And take them into the nursery. Georgina, put this on. And wash your face. Felicity, get off the bed. Why couldn't you do up his shoes for him?' She dumped the smallest child, Edward, on a chair. Now, until they were all ready, she wouldn't think, and what she said would be sharp, peremptory—the last commands before the battle was due to begin.

'Has Daddy come yet?'

'No. Socks, Georgina. Where's the comb?'

'You can have mine.' Charlotte offered one from the cupboard beside her bed; she was the only child to possess a comb of her own, and washed it in the bath every night.

'I don't see why he has to come home for your party. He didn't for mine.' Georgina was resentful, turning her drawer upside down for socks.

'Because,' Charlotte said, 'my party will be much nicer than yours. Yours was awful. Everyone said so.'

'They didn't!' She lunged, but Antonia caught her with one hand. Charlotte held out her skirt, pointed her toe, put her head on one side. 'Felicity hasn't got any pants on,' she said. 'I just noticed.'

'Georgina, find her some pants.'

'Why should I? Why can't Charlotte?'

'I've got to watch at the window in case they come.' Charlotte went quickly to the window and pressed her nose against it. Antonia found the pants herself.

'Tomorrow,' Charlotte sighed, her breath steaming the dark window, 'we shall have some peace.'

'Why,' Georgina asked truculently, 'tomorrow?'

'Because the babies are going away, silly. Mummy's taking them to Liversey, aren't you?'

'Yes,' Antonia said. 'Where's your slide, Georgina?'

'But how long will you be away?'

There was a second's calm, silence, lasting only as long as it took to draw a breath. During it Antonia looked down at her eldest daughter's face, raised so that she could push the slide into the straight, chopped hair. The face was troubled, the eyes contained a faint, hardly perceptible shadow. Antonia put in the slide. 'I'll be back in the evening.'

Georgina said urgently, 'I hate parties. I hate them.'

But it was too late, Antonia had already turned away. Charlotte said, 'Don't come, then—nobody asked you,' and at the same time the bell rang and she flew out of the door and they heard voices, the door shutting, Charlotte asking primly, 'Shall I hang up your coat?'

'It's started,' Georgina said.

They looked at each other over the heads of the small children, who were standing waiting to be told what to do. In both of their faces, although they did not recognise it, was the same look of hopeless alarm.

The Paintons' marriage, in a hot August thirteen years ago, seemed to them so long ago that the wedding photograph in the dining-room had become, to Antonia, almost a curiosity. Peering into it, she could detect her parents, younger, stronger than they were now, but wearing the same sort of clothes that they might wear in a few years' time to the weddings of their grandchildren; their faces, wrinkled against the sun, were prematurely old. The two people she could not recognise were herself and Mark. She did not remember having a round, solemn face with so much straight hair hanging on each side of it; she couldn't remember how it had felt to be so fat, to have so much flesh on her breasts and hips; her hand, lying on Mark's sleeve, the new wedding ring pushed over the plump knuckle, bore no relation to her hand now, which was thin, with tiny lines where the skin had not tightened over the bones. She had no memory of her hat or where she had bought it, or of the short-skirted, wide-shouldered suit, of which, presumably, she had been very proud. The only thing she remembered was something that couldn't be seen in the photograph: under the suit, against the unfamiliar body, she had worn a pair of black cami-knickers covered in small gold stars.

Mark had been thin. She remembered clearly the thinness of his chest and shoulders, and his suit was still hanging in the wardrobe, frayed and polished with age. The suit alone proved that the photograph was real. The sun had been shining, the champagne warm, the guests mostly unknown to her, and Antonia, ten years older than Charlotte was now, stood with her lashes lowered on to smooth cheeks, clutching flowers which had been picked that morning from the garden.

The smiles, the expressions, the clothes, the attitudes were all mysterious and enigmatic, a puzzle to which she no longer had the key. Perhaps that day on the lawn she had been thinking, as the camera clicked and her skin prickled in the new clothes, of something different. Certainly she hadn't thought of these years, these children, this fortress, which, though containing change and growth in itself, had been built to last, unaltered as they grew older, until they diminished inside its strong walls; until, at last, they died.

She knew this now, accepted it as someone accepts the fact that they will never see Tibet or Greenland or talk to pygmies in an African night. There was so much to do, so much coming and going, arriving and leaving; so much activity, eating, digesting, dressing, sleeping, being ill. The landscape of their lives appeared like the surface of an ant hill, seething with small, agitated movement. In the night their breathing was like a wind in the house. Lately, listening to it, Antonia had begun to hold her breath, trying to create for herself a little space of silence, of immobility.

'My father will be here soon. Then we can play the gramophone.'

Charlotte's friend, the first to arrive, looked at her uneasily. 'Is it a radio too?'

'It's a radiogram. We had it moved in here specially. Of course, we have a portable too. Would you like to look at the records?'

Gingerly, without enthusiasm, the little girl began picking through the pile of records. Charlotte sat down in an armchair on the other side of the room, spreading her skirt over the arms. Although there was a roaring fire, the big room was cold, fog drifted high across the ceiling, round the peeling cornices; the big gilt mirror over the mantelpiece was misty. The two children were silent for a few minutes. Only this morning at school they had been staggering round the playground with their arms round each other's necks. Now, because of their dresses and the strain of the occasion, they were strangers.

'We have rather an awful person coming, actually,' Charlotte said at last. 'A girl called Annette. Not a friend.'

'Why's she coming then?'

'Mummy asked her. Her mother's dead. I could hardly say no.'

'No,' the friend said, 'I suppose you couldn't.' She looked at Charlotte with timid admiration. 'Not if her mother's dead.'

The telephone rang urgently in the next room. They heard Antonia running downstairs to answer it. The front-door bell buzzed and Charlotte got up slowly. 'Some more people, I suppose,' she sighed. 'I'd better let them in. Do make yourself at home.'

Antonia, waiting on the telephone, saw the child walking decorously down the long hall. She put her hand over the mouthpiece and called, 'Georgina! Come down!' There was a click on the other end of the line and Mark's voice saying, 'Hullo? Antonia?'

'Yes, just wait a minute——' She put the receiver down on the desk and ran to the foot of the stairs.

'Georgina!'

Edward and Felicity came to the top of the stairs and stood together, looking as though they were about to throw themselves over a precipice. 'She's locked herself in,' Felicity said. 'She won't come out.'

'Well, you come down, then. Bring Edward.' She hurried back to the telephone. 'Georgina's locked herself in the lavatory again and they're all arriving. Are you on your way?'

'I'm terribly sorry.' He sounded distant, unrecognisable. 'I can't make it after all. Something's cropped up.'

'But, Mark—you promised!' She was watching, round the corner of the door the slow, reluctant descent of Edward and Felicity. She knew that there was no point in arguing, that he was not going to come. 'You promised,' she repeated uselessly.

'I can't help it. You can manage, can't you?'

'Of course,' she said automatically. 'That's not the point. It's Charlotte.'

'I'll try and get back before the end. Good luck.'

'Thank you.'

She put the receiver down and stood still for a moment, leaning on the desk. With surprise, as though it were some unexpected treachery, she realised how tired she was. As though this was not enough, as she straightened herself and turned towards the open door, the wide, misty corridor, she felt something worse, something new that was almost terror. The children— her own and those who had just arrived—stood in a group, watching her. The light shone on their brushed hair, the hard satin bows, the polished bronze of their dancing shoes. They stood curiously motionless, waiting. She stepped towards them hesitantly, like someone approaching a group of wild animals, feeling that they might suddenly charge or, on a signal from their leader, break away, swarm delicately and savagely through the house, destroying it.

CHAPTER 2

M ARK had said, 'Leave them to their own devices. They'll do what they like.' But she had, as she always did, prepared games. The first, the one that was meant to break the ice, consisted in pinning names to the children's backs; they then had to ask each other questions about themselves until, if they were sufficiently curious to get so far, they discovered who they were. The great thing was to stimulate interest, suggest questions they could ask, and when that failed to tell them with roars of laughter that they were Winston Churchill or Donald Duck; then to overcome, somehow, the looks of blank boredom with which this news was greeted. The whole thing, if properly organised, could drag on until it was time for tea.

Desultorily, the children wandered about the enormous nursery, the labels carefully pinned on net, taffeta and velvet. They looked at each other's backs and tittered a little and kept asking, 'Am I a man or a woman?'—the only distinction they seemed to recognise. Edward sat in a very far corner, watching them with a look of amazement. Felicity danced up and down, drunk, suddenly, with the party spirit. Georgina had not appeared. Antonia lit a cigarette and sat down by the gramophone. She switched it on, not because the game required music but in order to fill the bleak silences which fell after each child had asked, 'Am I a man or a woman?' A full, throaty baritone began, with infinite coyness, to sing 'Ring a Ring a Roses'. Charlotte turned round in despair.

'Oh, please! Not that. Anyway, I know who I am, so there's not much point.' She sat down, disassociating herself from the game. The others looked at her nervously.

'Even if you know who you are,' Antonia said, 'you can help the others.'

'Will Daddy be here soon?'

'He's held up,' Antonia said casually. 'He'll be here later.' She turned desperately to a fat child in shrimp-pink satin. 'I think you're a woman. In history. With red hair.'

'Rita Hayworth?'

'No,' Antonia said. She switched off the gramophone and changed the record. Out of the corner of her eye she saw Charlotte, tense, suffering, her fingers plaiting the artificial lace handkerchief she had bought for herself in Woolworth's. She said, not looking at the child, 'It can't be helped. He'll be here before the end, he said so. Cheer up.'

'He promised.'

'Shall we play Blind Man's Buff?'

'We play that,' Charlotte said scornfully, 'after tea.'

'Do we?' The children, following Charlotte's lead, had all given up and were staring at her accusingly.

They were all edging a little nearer to the fire, their bare arms blue with cold, their faces pinched and old-looking. She stood up, determined to say or do something outrageous; perhaps to tell them all to go home.

'The bell,' Charlotte said.

'It must be Annette. I'll go.' She escaped, hurrying into the cold hall, closing the door behind her. Through the frosted-glass panels in the front door she saw a vague, solid shadow.

She knew very little about him except that his wife was dead. He didn't come into the category of their acquaintances nor, exactly, of their friends. He was a man without a wife, a man with a child, someone who, with his married friends, belonged neither to the husband nor the wife, but was on equal terms with both. She knew he was forty, because she had read something about him in the newspaper: forty-year-old David Sangston, now directing a new film in Italy. He was not in Italy. Therefore, by now, he might be older. He was a vast man; her eyes seemed to take too long to travel across him; she looked away, embarrassed.

The fog swirled in; it was now quite dark outside.

'Oh. David.'

'I brought Annette.' He gave the child a little push forward, as though delivering her. Antonia couldn't see him properly. He was a large, indistinct mass retreating slowly down the steps. She said quickly, 'Will you—?'

'Yes?' His voice sounded muffled. He had turned, was looking towards her. She stood in the bright doorway, the child, wrapped and shapeless, beside her.

'Will you come and fetch her?'

'What time?'

'About—' She thought, frantically. How soon can it end? 'About six.'

'Right.' He seemed to hesitate, moving no further away. 'Having a good time?'

'Yes. Oh, yes.' She felt like someone on a desert island who sees a ship approaching, signals to it and then lets it go away, its lights moving farther and farther into the distance until, finally, they dip over the horizon and are gone. She asked, 'Are you going home now?'

The almost disembodied voice laughed. 'I've got to write some letters.'

'Oh.' There was always something irrevocable in the way people said they had to write letters: as though, of all things, it was the one that had to be done, could not possibly be postponed. She said, 'Well. See you later, then.'

'At six.' He moved soundlessly down the last step and into the shaft of light from the open door, which seemed to beat against a solid wall of fog. She saw him in an enormous overcoat, the collar turned up, his shoulders hunched, his hands in the pockets. She knew, suddenly, that he was not going to write letters.

'David—'

He turned again, his hand on the gate.

'Why don't you come in? I mean, if you could bear it. There's only me—and, of course, a lot of children. If you've got nothing else to do—' She was imploring him to come in. She sounded off-hand, casual, standing above him in the bright light, her hand on his child's shoulder.

'Only you?'

'Yes. Mark couldn't get away.'

'You mean you're coping with all that by yourself?'

'Yes.' She laughed nervously. 'If one could give them a drink or something . . .'

He came up the steps two at a time, accepting the invitation so suddenly, so completely, that it was as though they had both known all along that he would come in. She stepped back out of his way as he invaded the hall, shut the door, stripped off his overcoat and flung it over a chair.

'I'll take her things off.'

'I'll do it.' He bent, undid the buttons, unwound the scarves. The child underneath was small, her hair braided, wearing stout socks and a fair-isle sweater.

'She hasn't got a frock,' he said. 'Does it matter?'

'Of course not.'

'We brought a present for Charlotte. Where is it?'

The child showed a packet which she had been holding secretly behind her back.

'Let's give it to her, then. In here?'

In the nursery they were sitting about looking tense and unhappy; Charlotte was riding the rocking-horse, Edward was playing quietly with his bricks in the middle of the floor, the gramophone had stopped. They looked up without hope or interest, like prisoners whose sentences would not be over for many years.

23

'Hullo, Charlotte,' David said.

'Hullo.' She smiled, fluttered her eyelashes, slipped gracefully from the rocking-horse. 'Are you going to stay?'

'If I may.'

'Of course.' She saw the packet behind Annette's back and held out her hand. 'Thank you so much.'

'Charlotte—' Antonia said hopelessly.

'Why not? It's for her. Give it to her, Annie.' He spoke to his daughter coaxingly, with great tenderness, as though she might not understand what he said. Annette offered the parcel. The other children rose and edged nearer, grateful for this diversion. The string was undone, the paper came off, the lid was opened, and inside was a miniature box of face powder, a miniature lipstick, a small mirror with a gilt handle.

'Oh,' Charlotte said. She spun round, held out the box. 'Look. Look.'

'Oh . . .' they breathed, crowding nearer. 'Isn't it sweet, isn't it simply sweet . . .'

'Georgina will be *furious*,' Charlotte said. She did a little skip, transformed, radiant. 'Thank you. Thank you, Annette.' She turned to David and said, in a different voice, '*Thank* you.'

They were all smiling. The room, which before had been empty and echoing, seemed smaller and more crowded; the little girls stood expectantly round the large man, who looked down at them amiably, with confidence, taking his time. He glanced over their heads at Antonia. 'Why don't you go and get the tea? I'll cope with them.'

24

'You can?' She hesitated. They were waiting for her to go. They were all in love. 'All right.' She slipped out of the door and stood for a moment in the empty hall. Now she was no longer Georgina, locked upstairs in the cold; she was Charlotte. She flew down the stairs into the basement, turning on all the lights. From the nursery came the high, dragging whine of a trumpet, a tattoo of drums.

Antonia stood at the bottom of the stairs and shouted 'Tea!' with the full force of her lungs. Her mother had once given them a gong, but it had been buried in the sandpit and ever since it had been easier to shout.

The door opened upstairs and someone called, 'Did you say tea?'

'Yes. Come on.'

With the door open there was a sudden noise— shouting, laughing, screaming. She stood back and they came cascading down the stairs, jostling each other, running back, pushing forward, crowding into the small dining-room, where their skirts brushed against the fire, their plaits and bows hung perilously over the candles.

'Super, Charlotte!'

'I say, super tea!'

'Whizzo cake, Charlotte.'

Charlotte seated herself at the head of the table, in Mark's chair. 'I want Annette next to me here. Jennifer, you can come on the other side, if you like. Everybody else sit down somewhere. Can we begin?'

'Hasn't Georgina come down yet?'

'No, and she can stay up there for all I care.'

The children tittered admiringly. Georgina was in a higher form at school and none of them liked her very much. Antonia dealt with Edward and Felicity, tying on their bibs, giving them their jelly first so that they wouldn't complain.

'And David?' she asked.

'He's coming. He went to wash his hands.'

This produced another smothered burst of laughter. They looked pretty and wild in the candlelight, tearing at their food because of the gaps in their teeth, their hair untidy, they eyes savagely bright. She left them and ran up the stairs, along the hall, up another flight of stairs. The lavatory door was open, fog pouring in through the wide-open window. She slammed it shut and went into Georgina's bedroom. The child was standing in front of the fire, her feet apart, her hands locked behind her back, like an elderly gentleman interviewing a visitor. She looked round, her head on one side, as Antonia came in.

'Hullo,' she said. 'How's the party?'

'We're taking time off,' David said. 'Not very long.'

'Oh.' She glanced at him, then turned to Georgina. 'You must come down.'

'All right, all right.' She said to David, as though continuing a conversation that had been annoyingly interrupted, 'and he plays cricket terribly well. He was in the first eleven at his last school. And last summer he was captain. He made a simply enormous score. I

26

shouldn't be surprised if he doesn't play for England some day.'

'Indeed,' David said. 'He sounds some boy, this Daniel.'

'Yes, and—'

'Georgina!' Antonia said desperately. 'You must come down. It's so rude. You're only doing it to try and spoil it for Charlotte.'

'I'm not! I don't care one bit what happens to Charlotte's wretched party! I just don't see why I have to be there, that's all!'

'But—'

'Oh, come on.' He got up, put his hand on Georgina's shoulder. 'Let's have a look at them. There's no point in missing the food. He's playing rugger now, I suppose?' He was propelling her out of the room as Antonia, earlier in the afternoon, had propelled her into it. He didn't turn his head, or smile at her behind Georgina's back, and she realised suddenly that she had been expecting this.

'No,' Georgina said, as she went down the stairs. 'The boys play soccer, actually . . .'

Antonia turned out the fire and the lights and went into her own bedroom. She seemed unnecessary at the party. She shivered and drew the curtains; the light beat down on the huge, neat bed. At this time, before Mark came home and changed into his sweater and slippers, before she made up her face for the evening, the room was always unnaturally tidy, like a spare room into which visitors hardly ever came. She switched on the light over her dressing-table, touched her face with powder, her mouth with lipstick, tucked some stray hairs into the heavy, fair bun at the back of her head. How do I look? she wondered. Old? Still young? Attractive? The mother of four children? Pleasant? Dull? She peered at herself, trying to recognise herself, trying to make up her mind what she was, how other people would describe her. Mrs. Mark Painton. Antonia Painton. She switched the light off impatiently, smoothed her dress and went back to the party, following Georgina.

CHAPTER 3

THEY didn't seem to have noticed her absence. Georgina had sat down between Edward and Felicity and, safely buttressed by them, was enjoying her tea. David was leaning against the mantelpiece, watching. As she came in he turned and said, 'Hullo!' as though he hadn't seen her for some time, as though they had never met upstairs in Georgina's room.

'Hullo. How's it going?'

'Fine. They'll make themselves sick. It was nice of you to ask Annette. She doesn't often get outings like this.'

'It's nice to have her. Won't you have some tea or something? The sandwiches are quite safe, except the ones with brown in.'

'No, thanks. I never have tea. Cigarette?'

She took one out of his case, and he lit it with a candle, the flame wavering between them. Then he held the candle in front of the silver-framed photograph on the mantelpiece.

'This you?'

She laughed. The frame shone, but the picture inside was dark, indistinct. 'Yes. Our wedding photograph.'

He picked it up and held it nearer to his face.

'Your husband? Mark?'

'Of course.'

'One never knows. It doesn't look much like him.'

'No.'

'You look like this one here—' He gestured at Charlotte. 'Same eyes. Same shape of face. The little boy's like you too.'

'Yes. The others are both like Mark.'

'What were you doing then, when you got married?'

'Doing?'

'Yes. What did you do with yourself, before you got married?'

'Oh.' She had to force her mind back, to remember. 'Well, there wasn't much time to do anything. I left school, then I went to art school for a few months. I suppose to get me out of the way.'

'Painting? You wanted to be a painter?'

'Oh no.' She laughed again. 'I don't think I was much good.'

'Did you go on with it at all after you were married?'

'Oh, for a little while. Not long.' She turned back to the table, searching for something to do, but their plates were all filled.

'Did you keep any of these paintings?'

'A few. Charlotte, what about the cake?' She took a wax taper and circled it slowly round the top of the cake; one by one the nine candles came to life and started immediately to melt. The children were momentarily quiet, as though observing a fraction of silence for a year gone, never to come again. In the silence Antonia felt strangely desolate, cold, as though a door had swung open, letting in the night and the fog. She moved behind Edward's chair, putting her hand on his head, still young enough to seem insecure on the thin neck. The hair, like her own, was thick, fair, cold to touch.

'See the candles?' she asked.

He nodded. 'I will have a red birthday.'

'Red candles?'

'A red birthday.'

'All right.'

'You can't have a red birthday,' Felicity said. 'Silly.'

'I can!'

'You can't. Birthdays don't have colours, do they?'

'If he says so,' Antonia said, 'they do. Blow them out now, Charlotte.'

Charlotte stood up and filled her cheeks with breath, leaning over the cake. She let the breath out gently, expertly, and the candles died, leaving an acrid smell and drops of wax on the pink icing. Antonia licked her finger and thumb and pinched the black wicks. She gave Charlotte the knife and said, 'Wish.'

'I wish Daddy was here,' Charlotte said vaguely, then clapped her hand over her mouth. 'Oh—have I done it? I hadn't cut the cake, had I? It won't count, will it?'

'It does,' Georgina said. 'You can't have two wishes.'

'But I hadn't cut it—'

'You wished. You can't wish twice, can she?'

'Oh,' Antonia said desperately, 'she hadn't cut the cake. It wasn't really a wish.'

31

'It was! She said, "I wish Daddy was here." It's not fair if she has two wishes!'

'For heaven's sake,' Antonia said, 'it doesn't matter. Go on, Charlotte.'

'She's going to wish for a pony,' Georgina said scornfully. 'She always does. But it won't come true because she's wished already.'

'I'm not,' Charlotte shouted. 'I'm going to wish you were dead!'

'Oh!' Hardly realising what she was doing, Antonia turned to the silent man at the back of the room. He pushed himself away from the mantelpiece and came over to Charlotte, standing over her with his hands in his pockets.

'This is a problem,' he said. 'None of your wishes count if you say what they are. So Georgina won't drop dead. Anyway, you haven't cut the cake.' He put his hand over Charlotte's, holding the knife and pressing the point into the centre of the cake. They all held their breath. He waited, dramatically, then said, 'Now,' plunging the knife into the damp, spongy heart. Charlotte screwed up her eyes with effort. Georgina, her eyes wide, looked alarmed. 'There!' Charlotte said, collapsing suddenly into her chair. 'I've done it!'

Pandemonium began again, louder, more violent than before. They started pulling crackers, the table was heaped with scarlet paper, wreathed in smoke like a battlefield. Edward sat rigid, with his fingers in his ears. Felicity howled with terror and clung to Antonia's legs. David pulled crackers with them all, but did not, Antonia noticed gratefully, put on a paper hat. At last, clutching his hands, his coat, they dragged him upstairs. Antonia followed, wondering what was going to happen. Whatever it was, it would not, she knew, be what she had planned.

'Blind Man's Buff!'

'Let me be blind man!'

'No, me!'

'It's my birthday!'

The black scarf was tied quickly over Charlotte's eyes; she circled, beating the air.

'I hate this game,' Antonia said, edging warily away from the blind figure.

'Why?' he asked.

She laughed. 'It frightens me.'

Charlotte swooped, and Antonia ran to the other side of the room, picking up Edward on her way. The children, in delighted, savage mockery, poked and prodded Charlotte, rushing away from her as she stumbled towards them.

'Silly old blind man!'

'I'm here!'

'I'm here!'

At last Charlotte caught Georgina. 'It's a pig,' she said, as her hands felt Georgina's face and hair. 'It's a big, pink pig!' They screamed with laughter, hopping up and down. Georgina said, 'Don't be stupid. It's me. Give me the scarf.' She tied it herself and stood quite still in the middle of the floor. Her stillness seemed to subdue them a little; they couldn't taunt her in cold blood. Then Charlotte darted up behind her and pulled her hair. She turned, lunging at space.

'Silly old blind man!' Charlotte sang. 'Can't catch me!'

They all rushed at Georgina. She grabbed, but there was nothing there. She ran about wildly, but they were all too quick for her. Suddenly she turned and ran straight across the room, her arms held out, her head down. David seemed to step in her way, and she reached up and said, panting, 'That's easy,' and took off the scarf and looked back at the room, as though to make sure it was still there.

'Me?' David asked.

'Yes. Yes. Tie the scarf, he's sure to cheat.'

Antonia took the scarf and said, laughing, 'You'll have to sit down.' He sat down, and she folded the scarf, tied it tightly round his head.

'Can you see?'

'Not a thing.'

'You must come into the middle of the room.'

He held out his hand, and she took it and guided him into the middle of the room, then stepped back.

'Ready?'

'Ready!' they all shouted. They darted round him, quick and slippery as fish, running under his arms, crawling between his legs, eager and yet terrified of being caught. He grabbed somebody's sash and it came undone and he was left waving it in the air, looking huge, cumbersome, ludicrous. Edward, seeing that a grown-up was playing, took courage and dragged Antonia across the floor. Felicity took her other

34

hand and they ran together, Antonia bending double as the great windmill arms came towards her. Suddenly Edward broke free and began independently to caper round the room. David stumbled towards him, knocking over the fireguard.

'Mind!' Antonia shouted. 'Edward, mind the fire!' She let go of Felicity's hand and raced across the floor. The arm came down like a barrier; she held it, pushing against it. Georgina picked up the fireguard and set it upright. The arm bent, enclosing her.

For a moment, held there, her face against his chest, she was limp, captured. They were both out of breath, and she heard his heart, sounding like a drum in an empty room. Then his arm relaxed and his hand moved across her back, over her shoulder, up to her face. She could only see his mouth, and as she looked up at him the tips of his fingers touched her open lips and drew back, as though only then discovering that she was not a child.

'Antonia.'

'Right! Right! Mummy, you now!'

'No,' she said. 'Let's play something else.'

He pulled the scarf away from his eyes and was looking at her. She smiled. The scarf dropped to the ground between them. Georgina picked it up and Antonia heard herself saying, 'Put it on the bookcase, darling. It's Daddy's.' She turned, her voice rising. 'Well? What now?'

'I should think,' Georgina said strangely, 'Kiss in the Ring would be a good idea.'

CHAPTER 4

MARK walked in the dark between the lamp-posts; he walked near to the wall, and he was the only person in the road. Nobody saw him as he hurried through the feeble patches of light and on into the next long stretch of darkness. He had come up out of the brilliantly lit Underground with a group of people, men and young women, jostling up the steps with them, as unconscious of them as they were of him. All of them, the trainload, had dispersed into the fog, and each was now walking alone. He was glad to be rid of them, to be, for this short distance, by himself. When he rounded the corner and saw the final lamp-post he walked more quickly in order to overcome a vague but habitual feeling of dread.

The pattern of the Paintons' lives had developed without any effort on their part. They did things not because they were right or wrong, pleasant or unpleasant, but because there was no alternative. Except for the first nine months of their marriage there had never been a time when they could stay in bed until midday or go without lunch, fly to Paris at a few hours' notice or go to the cinema in the afternoon.

The children had imposed on them their own discipline and routine. They took it for granted that they should get up at seven and that their diet should consist largely of porridge, stewed apple and chocolate biscuits. Mark had never seriously questioned the fact that he had to grope for his razor on a shelf crowded with rubber ducks and celluloid fish, and that the soap, when he lay in the bath reading *The Times*, bobbed round him on a blue plastic raft. He depended through habit on the childish meal of tea and automatically ate two pieces of bread and jam and a slice of currant cake when he returned from the office, even if it was only an hour or so before dinner. Without tea, without pudding, without the alarm clock waking him on Sunday mornings, he would have felt obscurely cheated, deprived of something to which he had a right.

His feeling of dread, which he had never been able to master, was that something would have happened during the day to upset their lives; that when he got home something would have changed. He was sometimes clutched with anxiety like a sudden pain when he saw how easily people's lives could be destroyed.

And yet if he had asked himself, as he opened the gate, stumbled over an abandoned doll's pram, unbuttoned his overcoat for his key, why he felt this vague uneasiness he would have said that he was worried in case one of them had caught something during the day: measles, for instance—there was a lot of it about—or somebody might have rung up to ask them out to dinner, which would be a bore, or

Antonia might be in some small trouble—no coal or the char not turning up. He opened the front door and saw the overcoat and scarf on the chair, heard, through the half-open sitting-room door, Antonia's laugh stopping suddenly, as though cut off.

He looked round for somewhere else to put his coat and hat. After a moment, slowly and deliberately, he hung them on the banisters. Then, settling his cuffs, dropping his key back into his waistcoat pocket, he walked down the hall towards the sitting-room door.

'Mark?'

'Yes.' He went into the room. It was lit only by one table lamp and the firelight. He switched on the main light, and the harsh white walls sprang up like sentinels.

'Oh. Sangston. Good evening.'

'Hullo.' David got up from the armchair, held out his hand. 'I was invited to your daughter's party.'

'You were?'

'Annette was,' Antonia said.

'I see.' He bent and kissed Antonia, who was lying on the sofa. 'Is it over?'

'Yes.'

'Children in bed?'

'Edward and Felicity are.'

'Everything all right?'

'Fine.'

He turned to David. 'I shouldn't have thought children's parties were much in your line, Sangston.'

'I didn't until this afternoon. Now,' he smiled at Antonia, 'I shall go to more of them.'

38

'He was the greatest possible help,' Antonia said. She pulled herself up, raising her arms and tucking in strands of hair at the back of her head. 'We had trouble over the cake. Georgina was awful.'

'No,' David said. 'She didn't mean to be. It was something else.'

'What?'

'I think she feels that Charlotte gets too much attention.'

'Indeed?' Mark's face was impassive. He turned to Antonia. 'Any tea?'

'Yes. I'll put the kettle on.' She swung her legs off the sofa, but then, as though the effort had exhausted her, didn't move. She said, not looking at either of them, 'We were having a drink. I suppose you wouldn't like a drink.'

'But I haven't had any tea.' He wasn't complaining, merely stating a fact.

'No. I suppose you haven't.' She managed to stand up, smoothing her crumpled dress, stretching her body a little. She smiled at David and said, 'All right.'

'Not if it's too much trouble.'

'Of course not.'

'I can get it myself.'

'No.' She had taken off her shoes and wandered over to the door in her stockinged feet. 'Birthday cake?'

'Yes. Yes, all right.'

She still waited, her hand on the door. David said, 'It's seven-thirty. We must go.' He got up, towering, benign. 'Odd time to have tea, Painton. Still, I suppose that's why you look so fit. One should eat, they say, often and little.'

Mark glanced at him quickly. There was no malice, no contempt on the man's face; his expression was indulgent, almost caressing, like a woman who watches a favourite child being spoiled. He laughed awkwardly, rubbing the back of his neck where the stiff collar cut into the flesh. 'I suppose it is a bit late. I hadn't realised. All right, I'll have a drink.' With the decision he became bold, almost rough—the man he was during the day. 'What about you, Sangston? One for the road.'

'All right.' David sat down again. Antonia closed the door quietly and padded back to the sofa. Now they were Mark's guests and they waited silently while he mixed the drinks and handed them round, then sat down next to Antonia. 'So,' he said, with effort in his voice, 'it was a good party?'

'Yes.'

'Sorry I couldn't get back.'

She didn't say it didn't matter. There was another short silence. Antonia thought how strange it was that when she had been alone with David there had been no constraint. Now they were all three far apart from each other, stilted, uncomfortable, like strangers who will never meet again. Everything she thought of saying seemed pointless. She turned her glass round and round, watching it intently.

'How's the film business?' Mark asked stiffly.

'Oh, staggering along. How's the soliciting?' They

enquired after each other's work as though it were some disability which might by now have been cured.

'Not too bad. Still waiting for my partners to die.'

'What is the name of the firm?' David asked with remote sympathy.

'Blush, Monk and Painton,' Antonia said. 'Blush is ninety and Monk is mad, so Painton has rather a thin time. He keeps worrying about the day when he'll have to pay supertax.'

Mark shot her a look of reproof. With a sudden twist of her body in which only he recognised anger, she settled herself further into the cushions. He said, 'Isn't it time Charlotte went to bed?'

'It's early. In any case, I expect she would like to see you first.'

Obstinately, knowing that she meant he should have come home earlier, he did not move. She waited for David to get up and go, certain that he would. Instead, looking directly at her, deliberately excluding Mark, he said, 'Georgina says you're going down to the country tomorrow.'

'Yes.' She held out her glass to Mark. 'Could we have another drink? If you can call Essex country.'

'Don't be absurd,' Mark said. 'Of course it's country. There's no more gin.'

'There's a new bottle. I was brought up there, but I can't bear it. Cold and flat, always raining. Just like Liverpool Street. Stations are just like the places trains go to, don't you think so?'

'I hadn't thought of it,' David said, smiling.

'They are. Waterloo and Bournemouth, Paddington and Cheltenham Spa, Euston and awful places like Barrow-in-Furness, and then, of course, Victoria—'

'But from Paddington,' Mark said carefully, pouring the drinks, 'you go to Oxford, and from Liverpool Street you go to Cambridge, so what's the difference?'

'The difference,' David said, 'between Oxford and Cambridge, that's all.'

'Which is enormous,' Antonia said quickly. They were throwing this absurd conversation round and over Mark. She let it drop reluctantly, seeing him baffled. 'Of course, you don't want to go into it too much. It's only an idea. If we had a car—'

'There's no earthly point in having a car in London,' Mark said. 'Pure waste of money.'

'But it would be easier when we wanted to get out of London.'

'We never do. This is the first time any of them have been away by themselves. How often do we go away normally?'

'Once a year.'

'Exactly. And then we should have to have a pantechnicon to fit them all in. You, I suppose, have a car?'

'Yes,' David said apologetically.

Mark turned without comment to Antonia. 'What time is the train?'

'Half-past nine. We'll have to get up at six.'

'Why not let me drive you?' David said.

'Drive us? Where to?'

'Essex. Wherever it is you want to go.'

'Oh, don't be silly.' Antonia laughed, groped for her shoes, put them on.

'But I'd like to,' David insisted. 'Annette's going to my sister's tomorrow. I'd like some country air.'

'There's no country air in Essex.'

He turned to Mark, his hands spread out, appealing. 'But I mean it. Isn't it a good idea, Painton?'

'Well,' Mark said. He looked at Antonia. He was struggling in himself like a man trying to remember the language, the customs of some foreign country in which he had lived as a child. Normally, in his quiet, rather terse voice he would have thanked the man, refused the offer and thought no more about it. Now, for some reason, he found himself wondering why he was going to refuse. 'Well, it's very kind of you.'

'But, darling—'

'It would make the journey much easier for the children.'

'But you talk as though we were going to Scotland or somewhere! It's only an hour in the train—'

'Are you free, then? All day?'

'Certainly I'm free. But, of course, if Antonia would rather go by train—'

'It's not that. It's only—well, they're expecting to meet us. Besides, it would be so boring for you—'

'I wouldn't suggest doing anything that might bore me.'

Antonia looked helplessly at Mark. Unexpectedly, in some way she didn't understand, he had turned on her, was forcing her to do something that perhaps he thought she wanted to do. She asked, 'What do you think?', uncertain any longer what he thought.

He hesitated. He knew that the problem was simple, of no importance, and yet when he spoke it was as though he had at last wrenched away some small barrier or obstruction with which he had been wrestling for a long time. 'Yes,' he said. 'I think it's an excellent idea.' He repeated it, strongly, with emphasis. 'An excellent idea.'

Antonia said nothing. From the train window, safe, serene, she would have shown Edward the cows, the flat, winding water, flanked by willows; stepping from the train she would have seen her father on the familiar platform, the wind always beating round the little shelter, the signs swinging, clouds pouring across the immense grey sky. Going home had always been like this; as a child, as a young woman, it had always been the same. She looked forward to it, dreaded it and could not bear it to change. She turned, cold, polite, to David. 'Very well. It's kind of you. We needn't leave so early.'

'About eleven?'

'Yes.'

'Good. I'll collect Annie. We must go.' He got up, and they all went silently into the nursery. Annette was riding the rocking-horse, Charlotte lying on her stomach by the dying fire looking at an old volume of *Punch*. She jumped up and went to Mark, pressing her cheek against his waistcoat. David lifted Annette off the rocking-horse. The two men with their daughters became again strangers, the slight, masculine bond of the outside world broken. Charlotte said, 'Why didn't you come?'

'I couldn't. I had to go and talk to someone about somebody's will. I'd much sooner have been here.'

'It was a jolly good party, except for Georgina. Do you like my dress?'

'Beautiful.' He was horrified by her beauty, by the knowledge that it would never be tempered with much intelligence. 'How does it feel to be nine?'

She pushed him away, bored. 'Exactly like eight. Is Annette going now?'

'Yes,' David said. 'Where's Georgina?'

'Oh, upstairs somewhere.'

'She said she had to do her homework,' Annette said. It was the first time she had said anything. David looked at her fondly, then smiled at Antonia as though proud of the fact that his child could speak. She turned away, severe, strangely unhappy.

'Actually,' Charlotte said, 'she's writing her diary.' She crouched down in a chair, pressing her hand to her stomach. 'She writes beastly things about me.'

'Do you read it?' David asked, carefully wrapping Annette in her sweaters and scarves.

'Of course I do. That's what she writes it for. I've got an awful pain.'

'Too much tea,' Mark said. 'Come on, I'll take you up.' He lifted her. She lay fragile, her eyes closed, a look of deep suffering on her face. He carried her carefully along the hall, up the stairs, without saying goodbye. Antonia opened the front door. 'We'll see you,' she said, 'tomorrow.'

45

'Yes.' He seemed to want to say something else. Suddenly Annette spoke for the second time. 'Thank you very much for having me.' The wall of fog outside was green, impenetrable; they would move through it like ghosts to the other side, they would be swallowed up, gone for ever. Antonia said, 'Thank you for coming.' She felt that he was looking at her, puzzled, possibly hurt. He had no right to be hurt, to feel that he didn't understand her. Above all, he had no right to interfere. She said to Annette, 'Goodbye.'

They moved to the steps. 'Eleven o'clock, then?'

'Thank you.' At last she closed the door. She walked slowly back into the sitting-room and stood in front of the fire. She shivered, perhaps from tiredness, perhaps because of the fog that had crept into the house when the door was open. The children were quiet. For these few moments she was completely alone and as strange to herself as a woman seen passing along the street. Out there in the fog she would be nothing, she would have no existence. She was uneasy. She turned back to the room and saw herself reflected in the round convex mirror over Mark's desk—a minute, foreshortened figure in a great space of shadows. She ran out of the room and up the stairs calling, 'Mark!'

'Yes?' He looked up, surprised, from the book he was reading to Charlotte.

'Hullo.' She closed the door. The room was hot, clothes dropped all over the floor, the cat washing itself on Georgina's pillow. She said, 'I wondered where you'd all got to.'

'We've been up here,' Georgina said, 'for ages.'

She felt confident again. She knew what to do. 'Just look at this mess. I've told you not to have Thomas on your bed—for heaven's sake—'

The unknown world, with this house clinging to its side, turned steadily into the night.

CHAPTER 5

'It is a fine day, but last night it was very foggy. We had bacon and eggs for breakfast because Edward and Felicity are going to Granny's. Thomas was sick in the bathroom, Daddy got in a flap and everyone took great umbridge. He was sick because Charlotte gave him her cornflakes. Mummy says Edward is sure to be sick in the car. They are going in Mr Sangston's car, heaven knows why and he is sure to be mad if Edward is sick in it . . .'

Georgina sucked the end of her pen, sighed and looked out of the window. She believed that one day, when she was famous, she might be persuaded to publish her diary; or perhaps, after her early death, it would be found and serialised in the newspapers, together with her photograph: Child Prodigy. A Genius Lost To The Nation. She dipped her pen in the ink, thoughtfully drew a line round her thumbnail and continued: 'Charlotte has a pain. Ha ha. We are going to Madam Tussauds this afternoon with Daddy.' But it was no good putting what was going to happen. She had written about the party: 'Rotten, boring party except for Mr Sangston and the tea.' There was only one more thing she might put down. It was dangerous, because other people besides Charlotte might read it, and in spite of posterity she didn't really want anyone to know the secrets of her life. On the other hand there was Daniel. If she wrote something really startling in her diary he might be impressed. If she just told him about it he wouldn't believe her; he hardly ever believed anything she said. She bent lower over the notebook, writing quickly, the pen spitting on the coarse paper.

'This morning they locked their door. M was crying. I didn't listen, I couldn't help hearing. I think it's something about—' She hesitated, then wrote mysteriously, 'D.S. because yesterday she was being very peculiar.' Reading this, she had a moment of panic. Perhaps she ought to tear out the page. She would tear out the page this evening, when she had read it through a few more times. Someone was coming up the stairs. She stuffed the notebook into her pocket and began with strange energy to make her bed.

They had an electric clock by their bed because time was so important. A little red hand went round and round the clock face noiselessly, steadily, never stopping; the alarm, a kind of high-pitched groan, started at seven and went on until Antonia switched it off. Then she plugged in the electric kettle for their tea, and as it began to boil it became agitated, jumping about the floor, letting off a fantastic amount of steam. Mark never woke until she passed him his tea; then he raised himself a few inches in the bed, balanced the saucer on his chest and after a little while opened his eyes. The first thing he always saw was the pale brown liquid in the blue cup; he looked down into it blearily, as into a minute and muddy sea. Next he looked at Antonia's back. Except for a different night-dress it was always the same—smooth, with tiny hairs down the spine, her long, heavy plaits hanging over the side of the bed as she went through the complicated ceremony of switching on and switching off, plugging and unplugging. Finally he looked towards the window to see what sort of day it was going to be. During this time, until they first spoke to each other, they both collected their thoughts from the evening before, remembered what had happened yesterday and what was going to happen today, settled themselves again after the solitary and sometimes disturbing time of sleep.

On this Saturday morning Mark spoke first. 'The fog's cleared, anyway.'

'I had an awful dream.'

Mark found Antonia's dreams very tedious. He said, 'Oh? What about?'

'I don't know. Can't remember.' She turned slowly in the bed and put her head on his shoulder. He said, 'Mind my tea,' and lowered it carefully to the floor, bending his arm to hold her. Looking down at her face, he saw that her closed eyes were wet, tears held under the lashes. He said gently, 'What's the matter? The dream wasn't as bad as all that.'

'It's not the dream.' She put her arm across him, holding him tightly.

'What, then?'

She shook her head, pushing it against his chest, 'I don't know.' She hesitated, then said, muffled, 'I don't want to go away.'

'But you're not going away.'

'I know.'

Incomprehensible, irrational as the dream. He turned towards her. She straightened her body and moved against him. Her desire was sudden, unexpected; he responded to it with pleasure, but also with a slight, inexplicable feeling of embarrassment.

'I'll lock the door.' He got out of bed, and she heard the click of the bolt; then he shut the window; then, unmistakably, he was taking off his pyjama trousers. She shut her eyes more tightly, refusing to look, trying to prevent herself from thinking he is doing this, he is doing that, he is getting back into bed. He kissed her and lay still, his arms round her. There was no urgency, no greed; the moment of passion, drawn out by waiting, weakened and dissolved into the ordinary day. They lay loosely clasped, and Antonia heard the shrill, familiar sound of the children quarrelling. He pulled her towards him.

'Antonia.'

'Yes?' She opened her eyes, looking straight at him.

'What's the matter now?'

'Nothing.'

He moved his shoulders impatiently, clamped his hand over her breast. 'Well, then.'

'Oh. . . .' The distance between them was impassable. She pushed him away. 'It's late. There's a lot to do. I haven't finished the packing.'

'But—'

She moved away, almost savagely. The door handle turned and rattled, and she called out 'Yes?', but there was no answer. There would be no conclusion to this private scene; they would get up and carry it through the day; and when they met again in the evening they wouldn't refer to it because it was distressing, unpleasant to think about. He touched her again, tentatively.

'Tonia?'

She hesitated before she answered, steadying her voice. 'Yes?'

'Look here, what is the matter?'

'Nothing's the matter.'

'But I thought you wanted—'

She asked, 'What did *you* want?'

'Me? What do you mean?'

'That's exactly what I mean.' She sat up, doubling herself over her raised knees.

He said, 'You're behaving in the most extraordinary manner.'

'Yes.'

'Do stop being so hysterical.'

'Hysterical!' She shot up, blazing at him. 'I'm not hysterical!'

'You are, you know.'

'Oh!' She swung herself out of bed and struggled into her dressing-gown. She was trembling. She didn't even realise that she was sobbing until he said, 'What on earth are you crying about now?'

'I'm not crying.'

'You're behaving just like one of the children.'

She was unplaiting her hair, pulling at it blindly. 'You don't understand. You just think I'm a—dummy. That's all. A dummy.'

'No,' he said, 'I don't.'

'You think I'll put up with anything. Just because I'm your wife—'

He began, at last, to be angry. 'Put up with what? What are you talking about?'

'Everything's so dull, so dull.' She had, without meaning to, said what she meant. Saying it was like a blow on the face, a cold smack of sanity. She turned and said, 'I'm sorry. Of course it isn't true. I'm sorry, Mark.'

'I suppose Sangston is so very interesting—isn't that it?'

'Sangston? David?' She stared at him for a moment, then began to laugh, covering her face with her hands. 'Oh, Mark. Don't be absurd.'

He sat up in the bed, unsmiling. 'It's not absurd. It's quite reasonable. An attractive man, helping you out with Charlotte's party while I'm kept at the office—'

She looked up at him, pushing back her hair. 'You don't really mean this?'

'Of course I do. You've never behaved like this before. Last night you were—well, like a young woman.'

'But I am a young woman. At least, youngish. I'm not old, darling. My teeth are my own.'

'You're impossible.'

53

'I'm sorry.'

He got out of bed and unbolted the door. 'In any case,' he said, 'something's unsettled you. I can't think what else it could be.'

She had turned to the mirror and was putting up her hair, stabbing it with hairpins. 'I don't know what happened. I'm sorry. Forget it.'

He wouldn't forget it. He thought of the day without her, the ghastly prospect of Madam Tussaud's, the lonely and difficult meals; and all the time a sly, treacherous voice would be asking him whether he was growing old, incapable, whether he could any longer be called a man. He said, 'It'll do you good to go to the country. What shall I give them for lunch?'

'There's a shepherd's pie—you only have to heat it up. Georgina might do it.'

'All right.'

The door opened and Edward came in, naked except for a small straw hat belonging to one of Charlotte's dolls. 'Felicity called me everything,' he stated placidly. 'She called me a smelly jelly-baby and a copy cat, and she punched me and she smacked me.'

Antonia picked him up and carried him away. Mark went downstairs for the newspaper. In a few minutes they passed on the landing without noticing each other.

'They went off,' Georgina wrote, 'at half-past eleven. *Everything is back to normal* so I suppose what I wrote was only my imagination and anybody who reads this can jolly well TAKE CARE.'

CHAPTER 6

'Have you got the list?'

'Yes.'

'And the money?'

'Yes, dear.'

'Don't be too long. They may arrive early.'

'But the train—'

'They aren't coming by train, dear. By car.'

'Can't think how Mark affords a car.'

'A friend's car, dear. I told you.'

'First I've heard of it.'

'No, Alfred. I told you.'

'Oh. Very well, then.' The small old man pulled his cap down over his thin skull, wrapped his knitted muffler round and round, carefully put on his two pairs of gloves. His wife stood by, holding up the heavy, stiff duffle coat, hidden behind it, her arms breaking. With his back to her, he groped for the sleeves; a last, tremendous effort and she threw it on to him. He staggered under its weight, but she held him upright and nipped round to the other side of him, pegging him into it as deftly as she used to peg clothes on a line.

'Don't get cold, now.'

He shook his head. She slipped the shopping-book, in which she had written the list, into his pocket, handed him the basket. 'Don't forget anything. Don't forget the bacon at Platsbury's, not Finnikers. I've written it down.'

He nodded. She followed him out of the kitchen into the biting wind, her apron and her grey, soft hair blowing, her fur-lined boots slipping on the frozen mud. Slowly, his body snapping and creaking inside all his clothes, he wheeled his motor scooter out of the shed. It was a large green motor scooter with a windscreen: he felt no pride in it and always approached it with fear. He fitted the basket on to the carrier and with infinite caution mounted, his galoshed feet nervously feeling for the clutch.

'Don't go too fast,' she called against the wind.

He fumbled with a pair of ancient fur-edged goggles; when they were on there was nothing left of him. He pushed himself a few yards along the lane, and then, alarmingly, he was off, wobbling away between the high, swinging elms.

Mrs Levington hurried indoors. There was little difference between the temperature of the house and that of the garden, but at least there was no wind. She poked the fire in the range and decided to heat up the remains of the breakfast coffee. This was an indulgence, but for the moment she could not think of anything else to do. The chicken had been boiling since ten o'clock, the bullet-hard green sprouts were cleaned, the potatoes peeled. After she had drunk her coffee she would lay the lunch. She cupped her old, swollen hands round the mug of coffee and sipped it greedily, conscious that it was a luxury which Alfred, being carried precariously towards the town, could not share.

It was six months since she had seen Antonia. Like children, old people change rapidly. Six months ago Mrs Levington had been as Antonia had always known her—strong, vigorous, aggressively middle-aged. She had been in the thick of her private war, in which, one after another, the days were overcome, food reduced to meals, dirt trapped, mending wrestled with, disorder vanquished, victory gained. Compared with her husband, who had started to die on the first day of his retirement, she had been young. Then quite suddenly, just when she was shovelling the first coal of the winter for Alfred's fire, old age had arrived. In the dark coal shed, with a black mitten on her right hand, her boots slipping on the slack, her back bent, she had been stunned by her seventy years. When she came out of the coal shed she had been an old woman, certain of dying.

To begin with, it had made her unhappy. The first weeks of the winter had been full of regret. She thought continually of everything she had missed; thought, for the first time in years, of love; felt for the last time the pain of having no son. Then, as Christmas came nearer, she became reckless; squandered her savings in the local toy shop and knitted four warm cardigans in varying sizes for Antonia's children. She began wearing shawls in the evening and boys' football socks over her stockings to keep her feet warm. She became, with the release into old age, a little eccentric and happier than at any time since her marriage. She had written to Antonia and demanded to see Edward and Felicity, who would not notice that she was old. She didn't want any fuss, any pity. She didn't want Alfred to know, and this in a way was to pay him back for the life he had given her. Above all, Alfred must be kept in the dark.

But now that they were all actually coming, Mrs Levington felt a little afraid. Perhaps something would give her away. She was not wearing the socks, and her feet, in spite of the fur-lined boots, were bitterly cold. Her cooking, she hoped, was as good as ever; anyway, one couldn't go far wrong with boiled chicken and sprouts. She must comb her hair and take off her apron, but not before she had laid the table. And then there was something else she must do. She searched in her memory, groping and ferreting: she knew it was there, but it had gone, she couldn't find it. Nothing would betray her like something forgotten, some terribly essential thing like pudding. Bread sauce. She remembered it triumphantly, lit the gas, put the milk with its onion and cloves on to boil and reached for the stale loaf on the table. And custard. Now everything came crowding into her mind, confusing her. She left the table and went to the cupboard for the custard powder. Then she would need some more milk from outside the back door. She went to the back door and remembered bay leaves for the chicken. She had so much to do, and there was no time; she had wasted time dreadfully. She scurried up the garden, her body fighting against the wind.

When she heard the car draw up in the lane it was too soon, she could not get up. The kitchen smelt strongly of burnt milk, and she made a little gesture with her hand as though to wave it away, make a clearing in the smell and mist in front of her eyes. Her heart had grown too large, was pumping as though it might break through the thin, fragile chest bones, as though it would burst like a young chicken from its egg, leaving her shattered. She shook her head, saying out loud, 'Come along, now, there's no time for this nonsense.' She bent and, putting her full weight on her feet, stood up, leaning towards the table. The thick wood table, with its coarse grain, burnt rings and patterns of spilt ink, reassured her. She had known it for a long time, and its edge, clasped in her hands, was solid and friendly. She raised her head and saw through the kitchen window the roof of a green car parked in the lane. Reluctantly, sourly, her heart retreated to its place, its normal size; her forearms, still plump and freckled in spite of her age, relaxed as she stood upright; she fumbled with the knot of her apron and took it off without looking away from the window. At last she saw Antonia, Edward on one arm, leaning over the gate to unlatch it from the inside, pushing open the gate with her hip, waiting for Felicity, the wind blowing a strand of hair across her face. Mrs Levington stepped out with caution, with courage, as though crossing untried ground.

She stopped in the porch, knowing it would be unwise to go any further. She raised her hand against the wind and called, her voice carried away, hurtled and lost in the garden. Felicity came running to her up the path, arms and legs pistoning, hat awry.

'Hullo, hullo. Edward was sick.'

She bent and clasped the child, not so much to hold her but to steady herself after the violent impact. 'What,' she gasped, 'a big girl.' Then, holding Antonia and Edward both at once, she felt like a blind person feeling under their hand growth and imperceptible violence. When they moved away there were tears in her eyes. 'Oh, the wind. Where is your friend, dear?'

'He's getting the suitcases. Are we too early?'

'You know it doesn't matter what time you come. Your father went shopping, he's not back yet. What a big girl.'

'Here he is.'

The four of them stood in the green wooden porch, with its bundles of raffia and Mrs Levington's Wellington boots, watching David come up the path. He carried a suitcase in each hand and walked slowly, looking round, looking up, as though the sky were particular to this place. He is high, Charlotte had mooned last night, high, wide and handsome; she had slept with her box of face powder clutched to her stomach, where it hurt. Antonia felt a little twist, a wrench, as though something had been tightened in her chest. She said, 'His name's David Sangston,' and turned away, guiding Edward in through the door.

'I do hope they aren't too heavy, Mr Sangston,' Mrs Levington said. She held out her hand as though to take one of the cases from him. He looked down at her, smiling. 'This is a very beautiful house, Mrs Levington.'

She was almost flustered. 'You know, when you live in a place for so long you stop noticing it. . . . Do come in . . .' Chattering briskly, she led him down a short flight of stairs into a small, untidy room with a bright fire. '. . . If we could keep it up as it should be kept up. But as you say, it is a beautiful house, and so nice of you to drive them down, making the journey so much easier, but what a pity Edward was sick, I believe you can buy pills . . .' She was knocked breathless again by Felicity, Antonia and Edward slowly following. She began to sort them all out, delighted that Alfred was not here and that she had them to herself.

'You must be tired, darling. Sit down by the fire. As I was saying to Mr Sangston, you know you can buy pills for car sickness, wouldn't it be a good idea to buy Edward pills?'

Grateful, obedient, Antonia sat on the stool that had been her train, dolls' bed, painting table; she sat with her skirt drawn tight round her thighs, her hands stretched out to the fire.

'Sit down, Mr Sangston. I'll get some sherry. Would you like some sherry?'

'Thank you, but can't I—?'

'No, no. You sit down and get warm. Antonia, give Mr Sangston a cigarette, dear.' She hurried away.

Antonia looked in the silver cigarette-box and found it empty.

'There aren't any.'

'Have one of mine.'

They whispered, smiling. She looked down, seeing the extravagant brown suède shoe, laced high to the ankle, placed heel down, toe up, on the threadbare rug; the narrow gabardine trouser-leg stretched out, at ease. She said, 'There isn't usually sherry.'

'Not for Mark?'

She shook her head. Felicity had found Mr Levington's chessmen and was placing them in a row on the fender. 'The sun,' she moaned vaguely, 'came along in the sky and all the houses fell down . . . oh, said the old woman, all the houses have fallen down . . . oh, the sun came along in the sky . . .' Briefly, over the crouching child, Antonia met David's eyes, speculative, amused.

'Here we are.' Mrs Levington bustled suddenly in with a tray. 'They wanted me to have South African, but somehow I didn't feel it was right, though I'm sure they do make excellent sherry in South Africa. Mr Sangston, perhaps you would draw the cork for me?' Mrs Levington had never lived in a world where corks were drawn, but it was one of the few things she felt to be indisputably a man's job. Not that she would have asked Alfred to do it. Alfred was not, in that way, a man. It gave her a little extra pleasure to hand the bottle to David with the corkscrew, to see him turn it into the spongy cork and, holding the bottle between his knees, draw it out clean and whole. 'Perhaps you would pour it?' she asked, prolonging the moment. He got up and poured the thin amber sherry into the stubby diamond-patterned glasses. In the room were all the colours that Mrs Levington loved and Antonia remembered: sherry, all the gentle unemphatic browns, beige and rust, faded orange, woody green, stone and biscuit. The sun shone palely through the dusty windows, between the faded linen curtains with their dying pattern of beasts and birds.

'And how is Mark?'

'Very well,' Antonia said. 'Rather busy.'

'Good,' Mrs Levington said, quickly dismissing him. She had never really warmed, as she put it, to Mark; she always felt, though could never really believe, that he preferred Alfred to herself. 'And the children?'

'Charlotte,' Felicity said, 'has a pain. She says it hurts dreadfully here.' She pressed her hands to her stomach and crouched in agony. 'But I expect she ate too much.'

'You gave her some medicine, of course?'

'Well,' Antonia said, 'actually, no.'

'I should give her some tonight. A really stiff dose. I always think Charlotte looks constipated. And how is Georgina's chest?'

'Her chest?' Antonia asked desperately.

'How is her chest standing up to the winter?' The question was mild and interested. She looked enquiringly, brightly, over her sherry glass, which she held untouched, as though it were something she couldn't at the moment find a place for.

'Quite well,' Antonia said. 'I mean, she doesn't cough much.'

'I do think she should have an X-ray. What do you think, Mr Sangston? Don't you think Georgina is very chesty?'

'Really, David wouldn't—'

'She is thin,' David said gravely. 'I shouldn't have thought there was any harm in having an X-ray.' As Mrs Levington, gratified, bent towards Felicity and the chessmen he smiled at Antonia. She felt a sudden loyalty towards her mother, the same feeling that she had had as a child when she brought friends home to tea who sniggered behind their hands. She asked, 'Can't I do something? Can't I help with the lunch?'

'No, no. There's nothing to do.' Mrs Levington was annoyed by Antonia's question. She was enjoying herself and forgot that enjoyment was something new, something that Antonia didn't know about. She settled herself back in her chair, legs neatly crossed, hands in her beige lap. It could only be a short time before Alfred came home, and she was determined to make the most of it. 'And what do you do, Mr Sangston? Are you a solicitor?'

'No,' David said. 'No such luck. I'm in films.'

'Films?' Her eyes brightened at the possibility of something disreputable of which Alfred would not approve. 'An actor?'

He laughed. 'No. I make films. I'm a director.'

'How interesting. Does that mean you take all the photographs and so on?'

64

'No. I have the ideas—but it's not as easy as it sounds.'

'I'm sure it isn't.' If he had said it was easy she wouldn't have believed him. Nothing, particularly in a man's world, should be easy. She smiled her approval of him, of Antonia for knowing him. She felt wonderfully well. This would be something to think about in the long evenings while Alfred slept over his library book: how she sat doing nothing on a Saturday morning with Antonia and the children and the nice young man, how she offered them sherry, the ebony knights gallant on the fender, polished brass and polished copper leaves, which she had preserved in glycerine in the autumn, reflecting the bright fire. She put her hand over Edward's, fat, splayed, like a doll's hand. 'And Edward—do you know any new songs?'

The child shook his head firmly. Felicity said, 'He does. About the spider.'

'Sing it to me, Edward.'

'I don't want to.'

'I will,' Felicity said, jumping up. She arranged herself quickly in an attitude for singing. Edward, furious, pushed her away.

'It's my song.'

'You said you wouldn't sing.'

'I didn't!'

'You did!'

Relentlessly, Edward began to cry. First his face went pink; then his mouth sagged down, opening wider and wider; then, at last, sound came out. Mrs Levington bent to comfort him. Felicity crouched

c

quickly over her chessmen. Relieved of all responsibility, detached from the old woman and the children, Antonia and David smiled at each other, shrugged their shoulders, mockingly covered their ears.

There was a momentary pause for breath, and they heard slow, unwilling footsteps coming down the stairs. 'Here,' Mrs Levington said, 'here's Grandpa.' Edward stopped crying immediately. They all looked towards the door, as though Mr Levington, creeping reluctantly and inch by inch into the room, was making a dramatic entrance in the nick of time.

CHAPTER 7

ANTONIA, touching the edge of the oak dining-table, found it sticky, her fingers drew back from an old smear of marmalade, felt the table leg and came up into her lap with the tips grey with dust. She looked sideways at her mother, who was carving the chicken, then, reluctantly, round the room. There was never any sun on this side of the house; the fabrics had not faded, the enormous porridge and green birds were still discernible on the dark rust curtains, the carpet, spongy as peat, was unworn. In her childhood the room had been the innermost glade of the forest, cold, dark, the furniture like trees. She had come into it fearfully, shivering, breathing in the dank smell of cold silver and furniture polish; she had crawled cautiously along the bottom shelf of the Welsh dresser, tracked, tense with anxiety, through the legs of the table, lain on her stomach behind the sofa and peered with one eye beneath its sagging belly. She knew the slats underneath the sideboard and which of the brass handles were loose and the paper peeling off the inside of the slipper-box by the fireplace. She knew more about the room than her mother, more than anyone else in the world, although she

67

had never loved it. The room had never, until now, changed.

'We have our meals downstairs now,' Mrs Levington said. 'So eating in here is quite an occasion. You have the wishbone, dear.'

'Thank you.' She took the heavy willow-pattern plate. However many children were present, Mrs Levington always gave Antonia the wishbone, contrived that she should find the lucky sixpence. Reassured, she asked, 'Have you any help, anyone who comes in?'

'They're so unreliable. Besides, with only the two of us, it isn't worth it. Mr Sangston.'

One by one they were receiving their plates, looking down at the food, undoing the hand-woven napkins. Mr Levington came last, unprotesting at his small and scrawny portion. He had spoken very little since his return. He had nothing very much to say. Antonia had long since ceased to be his daughter and was now a strange, grown woman with whom he had only the slightest acquaintance; the children, whose names he was never sure of, were mildly surprising, because he did not know why they were here, why they were eating his food, why they talked as though they intended to stay for some time. He supposed it was some plan of his wife's, but since all her plans were most carefully arranged to exclude him, he was not at all worried. Whatever happened, he knew the routine of his dying would not be disturbed; his meals, his fire, his bed would be ready as usual. The only person in whom he felt the slightest interest was

David. He couldn't be expected to know who David was, and he would never, he imagined, have to see him again. Therefore, leaning sideways out of the enormous cage-like chair, he directed his pale, spectacled eyes on the stranger.

'You know this part of the country well, Mr Sampson?'

'Sangston, dear.'

'That is what I said,' Mr Levington lied calmly.

'No,' David said. 'No, I don't. As a matter of fact—'

'Constable country, of course. You care for Constable?'

'Yes, I—'

'Personally, I find him a little anæmic. No life. I quite agree with you about that.'

'He is getting,' Mrs Levington whispered audibly to Antonia, ' very forgetful. You see, he means he agrees with *himself*. It comes of being alone so much.'

Antonia nodded. There was dust on top of the sideboard; she looked away from it, down to her knife, which had the initials A.L. engraved on the bone handle.

'My school knife,' she said unbelievingly.

'I found it in the attic. You have no idea what I found in the attic. I thought I'd get it tidied up, you know, just in case there wasn't another chance.'

'What do you mean?' Antonia asked quickly.

'I haven't been to the attic,' Mr Levington announced with faint pride, 'for fifteen, twenty years. Of course, your mother's been ferreting about up there. No good my offering to help.' He looked coldly at Antonia. 'Found some of your paintings, I believe. Pity you didn't keep that up.'

'Yes,' she said. For the first time she felt apologetic towards her father, realised how alone he was in a world of women and children. 'But, you see, I was hopeless at it.'

'What does it matter?' He was speaking directly to her, his spectacles shining out of the great chair, his thin fingers impatiently tapping the knotted brown arms of the chair. 'You didn't expect to be a Degas, did you? No, for your own pleasure. Something outside—' His right hand made a little circle. He could not bring himself to describe her life, her mother's life. 'Something achieved. You understand?'

'Yes,' she said. She picked up the sticky wishbone, turning it round between her finger and thumb. Raising her eyes, she saw David looking at her across the table. They were all, she felt, deliberately misleading each other, but they weren't doing it well enough. The pretence was thin and didn't disguise the sharp, awkward shapes of their real feelings. She said to Felicity, 'Pull it with me.'

'You know,' Felicity said, pressing her thumb against the flat end of the bone, 'God's hand is on your head every minute?'

'Who told you?'

The child thought for a moment, then said, 'I don't know. Shall I tell Edward?'

'If you like.' Antonia slid her thumb down so that her daughter would get the larger half of the bone.

Then, as they pulled, she regretted it, wondering whether, because of this, some extraordinary part of her life which should have started with the wish would never happen. Felicity turned to her grandmother.

'Are you going to die?'

Mrs Levington smiled. 'Of course,' she said.

'I thought so,' Felicity said. 'I'll wish for myself, then.'

It was Mrs Levington's invariable habit, when she had done the washing up and brushed the crumbs off the table and put the empty milk bottles outside the door, to climb upstairs to her bedroom, cover herself completely with the warm eiderdown and sleep. In Antonia's childhood this sleep had lasted for exactly fifteen minutes; it had been not a rest, not an indulgence, but a kind of physical exercise. As other people did deep breathing or touched their toes five times, so her mother slept, never exceeding a quarter of an hour, always coming downstairs brisk and braced, never yawning, never, apparently, unwilling to resume the day. So that when her mother said, 'Well— just forty winks, if you don't mind,' Antonia was not surprised. While they had been washing up, Mrs. Levington had asked all the right, the usual questions: she had indicated that both Georgina and Charlotte were due for an early grave if they didn't wear liberty bodices, a garment in which she had great faith. She had even suggested that she should have all the children to stay in the summer so that Mark and Antonia could have a holiday by themselves, without which, she insisted, Antonia would certainly collapse, or worse.

She had been, in fact, so normal that Antonia had no idea of her thoughts as, secretly hugging a hot-water bottle, she climbed up the stairs to bed. The truth was that in the last few months Mrs Levington had given up her exercise of sleep and had taken to it avidly, sleeping for hour after hour, waking only when it was time to get Alfred's tea. At night she slept lightly, often waking to read her library book or suck a barley sugar, but her afternoon sleep had become prodigiously deep—the front-door bell, the telephone, the alarm clock could never waken her. She decided that this afternoon the only thing to do was not to go to sleep at all. She would get into bed, yes; prop herself against the soft pillows and pull the eiderdown up to her chin, but she must not go to sleep. She took her book from the bedside table and opened it at random. She began to read about some boy at Eton, or could it be Harrow—she glanced at the dust cover, but, of course, there wasn't a picture on it—who had some trouble which, though dire, was not clear to Mrs Levington. She began thinking of Edward, whom she loved most. Edward and his troubles, the years ahead, the ageing of Antonia, the great length stretching out of life which she would never know. . . . The book fell and Mrs Levington slept.

Downstairs in his room, which had never, because of Mrs Levington's contempt for his activities, been called a study, Mr Levington also slept. He had nothing to wake up for, but his sleep, unlike his wife's, was disturbed and uncertain. His leg jerked, his head turned suddenly, his hands twitched; consciousness of time, of cold, of danger, perpetually disrupted his sleep, and when he woke he often didn't know where he was or who he had suddenly become.

Now, Antonia thought, it will soon be over; soon we shall be going away. She balanced one cardboard brick on top of another, waited till Edward knocked them down, then turned and lit a cigarette with a purple spill from a jar by the fireplace. She had never known any house except this and her own where there were always purple spills in jars by the fireplace.

She held the spill and watched the end blacken, curling up to nothing. The drawing-room faced south and was almost colourless; even the flames at last hissing up from the wet logs were practically invisible. Here were the photographs, the piano, the little cups of dried lavender and objects such as paper knives, candle snuffers, inkstands, which were never used. She said, 'They'll just be starting for Madam Tussaud's. Poor Mark.' She looked at the photograph of him on the piano, and added, 'We should have brought them, too, there was plenty of room in the car.'

'I'm glad we didn't.'

'Why?'

'Various reasons.' He leant forward and placed one cardboard brick on top of another; he had labourer's hands, carefully manicured. 'I only suggested bringing

73

you because I was pretty certain Mark wouldn't come.'

'Oh.' She was flattered and hurt by this separation from Mark. She said, honestly, 'I don't see why. Mark is more interesting than I am.'

He laughed, knocking down the bricks. 'You mean that?'

'Of course.' She was angry now, slamming the bricks down in a straight line, taking one from Edward. 'Mark is interesting. I knew that you'd be bored by coming here. It was kind, but I didn't ask you to come.'

'Mark,' he said gently, 'is a man.'

'Don't you like men?'

'Naturally, but I don't go out of my way for them.'

'Why for me, then?' To you, she meant, I am almost a man; I am not, at any rate, a woman as far as you're concerned. She wanted to be told what she was, and yet dreaded his answer because it would, she felt, be final.

'Let's look at your pictures.' He got up and wandered round the room, away from her. 'Where are they?'

'I suppose they're still up in the attic.' He had not answered her question, and a sudden weariness came over her, a slight disgust with herself. Whatever she was, nothing would change her now. If Mark had been jealous it was only that in the bitterness of their quarrel he had confused her with someone else, and she had wondered for a little while whether it was true, whether she was someone who might, even now, cause him jealousy. It wasn't true. She said dully, 'We can't go up there.'

'Why not?'

'Oh, it s so dirty. Besides, the pictures aren't worth looking at.'

Felicity came out from behind the sofa, where she had been playing cards. 'I want to go to the attic,' she said.

'No.'

'I want to.'

'I want to', Edward echoed vaguely, and prepared himself for tears.'

'But it's so stupid. There's nothing there.'

'I want the attic,' Edward said ominously. 'I want to go to the attic.'

'Oh. . . .' She stood up, not looking at David. 'All right, then. But be quiet. Granny's asleep.'

She took Edward's hand and they crept up the stairs, Felicity and David following. The way to the attic was through her old bedroom. The brass doorknob was loose and the door still difficult to open. She pushed it and it swung back, showing the deserted room, dust thick on the dressing-table, curtainless, carpetless, a room without life. Antonia caught her breath. It was as though for an instant she had seen the rooms of her own house neglected, silent, empty of children. She said slowly, 'I thought Felicity would be sleeping in here.'

'Oh, no,' Felicity said grandly. 'I'm sleeping in the spare room.'

75

'Another spare room?' David asked incredulously.

'Of course,' Felicity said. 'You know there are hundreds of rooms.'

Antonia unlatched the attic door. The stairs wound darkly up, smelling of dust, of leather and birds' nests. They could hear the cistern dripping, but otherwise everything was silent, the house wrapped in sleep. The children, a little frightened by the dark, stepped back, waiting for the grown-ups to go first. Antonia led the way. The attics ran the whole length of the house, and thirty-five years ago Mr Levington had had them re-floored; he had thought then that the attics would be admirable for clockwork trains, footballs, roller skates; he had secretly dreamed how he and his son would come up here to escape the endless clattering of dishes, humming of carpet sweepers, the steaming and bubbling of one more inescapable meal. But there had been no son. Mrs Levington had suggested once or twice that they made a studio for Antonia up there, but by that time he had lost interest. The sturdy floors were a memorial to Mr Levington's only personal dream.

Up here they were among the wind and the sky, the rafters creaked, and every moment some tiny part of the house was dislodged—a flake of plaster, a splinter of wood, a cluster of dust. The attic was divided by a thick wall, in the middle of which there was a wide, doorless archway, so that, standing at the top of the stairs, you could look through the archway down the whole length of the attic, with its shrouded trunks like tombs, the dim, statuesque shapes of crates and tea chests, to the high window at the end, where ivy had struggled through the rotting wood and densely filled a hole in the glass, hanging two emaciated tendrils down the inside wall.

'I shall never find them,' Antonia said. 'Don't you see?'

'It's dark,' Edward said. 'It's dark.'

'Baby,' Felicity said, and did not move.

David lit his cigarette lighter; the tiny flame increased the darkness, which before had only been twilight. He walked away, leaving them standing at the top of the stairs.

'I think we'll go down,' Antonia called.

'Hold on. Here's a candle.'

Beyond the archway the further part of the attic glowed with a small, wavering light; David's shadow loomed gigantic on the wall, then spread out behind him as he came towards them holding a candle in a saucer. Felicity said, 'Ooooh,' and stepped back, treading on Edward's toe. Above the little flame David's mouth stretched in a reassuring smile, infinitely menacing. Edward screamed and clutched Antonia's skirt; it was something he would never, in the whole of his life, forget. Antonia said, 'Let's go,' and turned, with Edward clinging to her knees.

'Don't let's go.' He was a magician, a genie, the whites of his eyes gleaming. 'There's a box of dolls. Dozens of them.'

'Dolls?' Antonia asked. For the first time in nearly thirty years she saw them, momentarily, in her mind: Bluebell, with hair and a cracked face; Anthony,

77

slashed with the nail scissors; Marigold and Murphy; the fingerless hand of Ethel, all thrown into a common grave.

'A doll's house,' he said. 'Come and see.'

They still hesitated. He said, 'It's very large. Perhaps you could take it downstairs.'

Felicity looked down and saw daylight coming through the open door, and a sensation of the whole house, light and quiet and full of ordinary things, beneath her feet. She said, 'I don't care,' and stalked proudly into the attic. Antonia lifted Edward, and they all followed Felicity.

The dolls were there, the dolls' house was packed with toys. 'Why did she keep them?' Antonia asked, squatting down and peering into the little rooms stacked with boxes, skipping-ropes, paint-brushes held with rubber bands. 'Why didn't she give them away? Or to us?' Her mother was becoming more of a mystery. There were more candles in saucers, used by Mrs Levington when she was tidying up. In a few minutes the attic burned like Christmas, Felicity and Edward rifling the neat parcels. Antonia stood up, a broken Hussar in her hand. The candles were placed round the children on the floor, and David and Antonia, standing, were beyond the ring of light.

He took the Hussar from her and turned it over in his hand. 'Yours?' he asked.

'Yes.'

'The paintings,' he said.

'Oh.' She picked up a candle. 'There's a box at the top of the stairs. Perhaps in there.'

78

She walked back down the long attic, through the archway. He followed her and took the candle from her without speaking. She bent over the high brown trunk with A.L. painted in black on its lid. Suddenly she stood up, looking away from him through the archway, seeing the shadow-play of the children and the house on the wall.

'The clasps are rusty. I can't undo them.'

'It doesn't matter.'

He put the candle down and bending, without touching her with his hands, kissed her mouth. The kiss was as hard, as cool as the back of her hand against her mouth. She did not move, but stood with her arms at her sides, looking at him. He asked, almost coldly, 'You mind?'

The words, the quiet, controlled voice were far away—echoes in an immeasurable cavern of thought. He lifted her towards him, opening her lips, forcing his way into her until she was part of him. When he let go she stepped back, uncertainly making a little gesture such as a woman might make who, searching for someone, goes into the last room and finds it empty.

He picked up the candle and turned away. She said, 'David—' He disregarded her, calling to the children. They appeared in the archway, very small, the glitter of light and toys behind them.

'Blow out the candles. We're going downstairs.'

'Where's Mummy?'

'Here,' Antonia said, coming forward. 'I'm here.'

Their calm, preoccupied eyes looked at her, then glanced indifferently away. They did not see her at all. They only saw someone whose age, like that of the world, was more than they could grasp, someone of great durability who belonged completely to them.

CHAPTER 8

THE small procession had entered the green marble hall of Madame Tussaud's, was standing at the foot of the stairs, looking upward. The agony of it, to Mark, was now sharpened with surprise. He was, he realised, actually here; the halls and the kings, cabinet ministers, champions, were now inescapable. He looked helplessly at Georgina.

'Where do we go first?'

'We have to go up here. There's no choice.'

'Charlotte?' He looked for Charlotte, who was sitting on a small gilt chair. 'All right?'

She raised her head. 'My pain is worse.'

'Perhaps we should go home?'

'No.' She got up, her arms pressed to her waist, carrying her pain with care. 'It's all right. The Chamber of Horrors . . .'

'Mummy said we weren't to go in,' Georgina said, swinging round on the banisters. 'But I suppose we can.'

'Since the babies aren't here,' Charlotte said. Mark started up the stairs without answering. He was, perhaps, the most conscientious and uncomplaining sightseer in London. There was hardly a museum, exhibition, gallery or ruin where he had not been. On wintry Saturday afternoons he had vaguely explained the Elgin Marbles, tied the shoe-laces of children sitting on Egyptian tombs, peered at stones and boots and little antiquated combs, lifted Felicity to touch a Rodin, and prevented by a hair's-breadth the destruction of a Degas. He had plodded round the Museum of Hygiene and Museums of Local History and Antiquity, exhibitions of wheels and tea and dry-rot and the incunabula of obscure religions. But he had a horror of waxworks. He had not been to Madame Tussaud's since, as a child, he had been carried screaming into a taxi, where he had been sick. He remembered the beady eyes of his aunt's fox fur and the driver saying it would cost ten shillings to have the cab cleaned. With greying hair, shoulders a little bent, his daughters climbing behind him, he felt again the sense of anger and insufficiency: the day, for the second time, had him off his guard.

A slow, subdued crowd moved round the dark hall. Mark and the children stepped into place, shuffled forward. The intent wax faces of elder statesmen, double chins rigid, whiskers unmoved by breath, stared beyond them, never meeting their eyes. Charlotte took Mark's hand. 'Who are they?' she asked. 'Anybody I know?'

'It's the Queen,' Georgina said carelessly. 'Can't you see?'

'I should think it's not like her.'

'You don't know what she's like, do you?'

'The Conservative Government,' Mark snapped. 'Look at Winston Churchill.'

'I have looked at Winston Churchill,' Georgina said. 'What about the Sleeping Beauty?'

They watched the wax breast rising and falling. Mark consulted his guide book, holding it right under his eyes, the crowd jostling him. 'It appears,' he said, 'she was guillotined at an early age.'

'How early?' Georgina asked.

Charlotte said quietly, 'I feel sick.'

'Was she young?' Georgina asked, snatching the guide book.

'I think we should go home,' Mark suggested desperately. 'You can't be sick here.'

'No,' Charlotte said. She winced away from his hand. 'I don't want to go home. It's just stuffy in here, that's all.'

'Perhaps it's better upstairs. The writers and so on.' They followed him obediently out of the dark, climbed again up the stairs. They did not mind which waxworks they saw provided that Mark showed interest; they could not have borne it if he behaved as though he had come for their pleasure and not his own.

'Kipling,' he said. 'Remember the Jungle Books, Georgina? He was a small man.'

'Yes,' she said, looking moodily away. 'I can see that.'

'And there's Byron. You know Byron?' he asked bitterly.

'I know he had a dog. Where's Charlotte?'

She was lost. No faces could be seen but the slightly sweating wax faces; the living crept forward in semi-darkness, their eyes flickering over the dead glass eyes. Mark stepped out of line and stood peering, searching. His irritation and anxiety became suddenly unbearable, like a very tired man, tired almost out of his senses. This losing of Charlotte was the last straw. He repeated in a high, angry voice, 'Where is she? Where has she gone?' Georgina stood quietly by, her hands in her pockets, looking down in case she should see Charlotte and spoil the moments of panic. 'Perhaps,' she said, 'she has gone outside to be sick.'

'Go and see.' He lunged across the floor, pushing unyielding bodies. He saw a handbag fall to the ground, slowly open and pennies running gracefully away on their rims, powder compact, keys, purse sliding gently out of the black leather envelope until they lay displayed, as though with some purpose, in a small clearing. He bent, then raised himself again, knocking sharply against an outstretched arm. A woman said, 'Damn,' and trod on his foot, her high heel spearing his week-end suèdes. He said, 'Look, really——' and submerged himself, groping with held breath for the bright, slippery objects. A voice said, 'It's all right, Painton. Don't give it a thought,' and looking up he saw, within two inches of his own face, the large, benevolent face of a Queen's Counsel named Roger Teasdown.

'So sorry,' Mark said. 'Such a crowd.'

'Not to worry,' a woman said. 'Positively not to worry.'

Sitting on their haunches, they both looked up. The dazzling smile was sent down to them as though by some form of wireless. They bent again to their task, their large hands incompetently scooping and stuffing the handbag. At last, with difficulty, they stood up.

'My wife,' Teasdown said, pushing the handbag into her arms. 'Mark Painton.'

The brilliant message was again despatched but not, by Mark, received. He was again searching the crowd. Seeing now not even Georgina, he turned and made a vague, apologetic gesture. 'So sorry,' he repeated, 'the children—'

'What an enchanting place,' Mrs Teasdown whispered, as though he alone should know the enchantment she had perceived under the vizor-like brim of her hat. 'I was, in fact, saying to Roger. Absolutely enchanting.

'Georgina!' Mark called feebly, turning his back on Mrs Teasdown.

He was now in a state which had become, over the years, part of his nature. He was obsessed, entirely concentrated, the Teasdowns and the waxworks meant nothing to him. He was beginning to move away when Georgina appeared.

'There you are. She has been sick.' She said this in a clear, expressionless voice. 'You'd better come.'

'Where?' Now Georgina was back he realised, for the first time, the Teasdowns. His eyes slid desperately across the monumental chest which he had seldom before seen unrobed. 'Where is she?'

'Outside. On the stairs.'

He stared at Mrs Teasdown. 'Charlotte,' he muttered. 'One of the children. She's not been well.' A miracle, then, would have been for Mrs Teasdown to run outside, as Antonia would have done, and deal with the thing. The lower half of her face—all that was visible—remained unmoved except for the mouth, which said, 'Poor mite,' with brisk repugnance. Mark was angry. He turned away and hurried, with his bent, almost jumping stride, across the dark hall, Georgina following him.

Charlotte was sitting on the stairs, and someone had pushed her head down between her knees so that she looked deformed, staring at the carpet, her back bent double, her neat, white-socked feet set wide apart. Georgina stood some way away, glancing at her with the same furtive curiosity of the crowd coming up the stairs. When Mark shouted at her she came unwillingly, revolted by the smell of sickness.

'Go down and ask them to get a taxi.'

'Ask who?'

'Anyone, for God's sake! Have some sense!'

She ran down the stairs, and Mark picked Charlotte up, carried her down; her face was pale and sweating, her fingers twitched and grasped his coat, her head turned violently away from him. He was reminded of the few minutes in which, some years ago, he had seen Antonia in labour: the same sense of hostility, of obsession; he asked, 'Have you still got a pain?'

She nodded.

'Soon have you home now.'

She nodded again, not caring. In the taxi Georgina asked, 'Do you think she's ill?'

'We'll get the doctor.'

'Hadn't you better phone Mummy?'

'She'll have left by now.'

'She won't. They won't leave till after tea.'

'She'll be home by six, anyway.'

'They might stop on the way. You never know.'

'Why on earth should they stop on the way? Will you stop arguing?' His resentment against Georgina blazed momentarily, shocking them both. His emotions about his children were charged with this unsuspected violence, as though he spent on them the feelings which might have been distributed over friends, enemies, even perhaps a mistress. For Georgina he felt a competitive, almost antagonistic love. She was the sister he had never had, the awkward, angular child impossible to think of as a woman, and for this reason infuriating, stinging him into spite, even at times cruelty. He gently pushed Charlotte's hair off her forehead and looked stonily out of the window. Georgina pulled the fluff out of the inside of her pockets and rolled it between her fingers into hard little balls.

Nevertheless, when Charlotte was in bed and the doctor on his way, he tried to telephone Antonia. Mrs Levington's voice, as always, sounded as though everything she was saying into the telephone was secret.

87

'Oh. Mark. Antonia's left. They went about an hour ago.'

'All right. That's fine.' Then, with an effort, 'How are you?'

'Oh, very well. Would you like to speak to the children? They're just here.'

'Yes—yes, of course.' He waited impatiently, finding a cigarette, holding the match-box in between his knees as he struck a match. There was a great deal of murmuring and heavy breathing and finally, breathless, 'Hullo . . .'

'Hullo. Who's that?'

'Felicity.'

'Oh. Are you having a nice time?'

'Yes.'

'Being good?'

'Yes. Edward's here.'

More scuffling, then a diminishing wail; Mrs Levington's voice, secret and brisk, 'Edward doesn't want to speak on the telephone. Are you quite well, Mark?'

'Yes, thanks. Charlotte's got a slight pain, nothing much. I'll expect Antonia in about an hour, then.'

'Oh yes, I should think so. Give her some magnesia, just a teaspoonful. Mr Sangston seems to have a very fast car. So nice of him to bring them down.'

'Yes.'

'Well, we must get them off to bed now. Good night, dear. Give Georgina and Charlotte my love.'

After he had telephoned he poured himself a drink without realising that he had had no tea. Georgina had disappeared, probably up to the attic; Charlotte was quiet. He felt restless, sure that there was something he ought to be doing, but not knowing what it was. The house, with only the three of them in it, seemed empty, unnaturally silent. He turned on the wireless and turned it off again, picked up an evening paper and found it was yesterday's. His thoughts moved uneasily round an indistinct feeling, the shape in his mind of trouble, disturbance; possibly even danger. How could he keep all this together? How prevent the weakening, the unmistakable tremor that could come with something so slight as a child's pain, the departure of two children, Antonia's shortest absence? To come out with it, then, what was he afraid of? That Charlotte was going to die? That Antonia had gone off with Sangston, never to be heard of again? In that case, he said to himself, I should . . . He gave himself another drink, walked the length of the room, screwed up his eyes at a Matisse print which seemed unexpectedly horrible: faceless woman with a table-leg piercing her thighs, yellow floor covered with the footprints of a hundred jumping cats. Why the hell we ever bought it . . . Charlotte was not going to die. Antonia would not go off with Sangston. Everything would remain the same. The failure of the morning, which already, perhaps for years, he had come to expect and dread, would be repeated again and again, but they would not do anything about it, nothing could be done. Everything, he thought, looking at the print, a snapshot of Felicity, a small Dresden plate propped up on the mantelpiece, will remain the same.

He banged his glass down on the mantelpiece with such force that the plate toppled and slid down on its back. He felt a jump of fear, an overwhelming relief that it had not broken. He put it back, straightened the Matisse, rubbed the mark of the glass off the mantelpiece with his handkerchief. When the front-door bell rang he put on his jacket before answering it.

The doctor, muffled in an enormous woollen scarf of some provincial rowing club, stepped inside, rubbing his hands together. 'Foggy again,' he said. He was a young man with a thatch of long black hair and beautiful eyes. Mark had no knowledge of his skill or lack of it, but distrusted him for his appearance.

'Well, what's the trouble?'

'It's Charlotte. She's got a pain and she's been sick.'

'I see.' The doctor went up the stairs, avoiding, from past experience, the loose stair rods. 'Any temperature?'

'I don't know. My wife's away. I haven't taken it.'

Charlotte was lying on her back, her hands clasped over her stomach. She was pale, but apparently calm. She looked at the doctor through her eyelashes, without smiling.

'Now then,' he said, 'what's all this?' He spoke the jovial bedside phrases with a kind of hesitant melancholy. 'Pain? Show me where.'

Charlotte showed him, uncovering a stomach still round and swollen like a baby's. Mark, sitting on Georgina's bed, looked at the floor.

'I see,' the doctor said. He put a thermometer in

Charlotte's mouth and picked up her wrist. 'Your wife away for long?' he asked.

'No. Just for the day. She'll be back any minute.'

'I hope she wasn't driving. The fog's thicker than ever.' He dropped the wrist and opened his brown fibre case. When he looked at the thermometer he said, 'Yes,' and sat down on the edge of the bed. Charlotte watched him, expressionless. Mark followed his hands moving across Charlotte's stomach, touching, resting for a moment, springing suddenly away. 'That hurt? That? Here?' Sometimes Charlotte shook her head; sometimes she nodded; twice she stiffened and twisted her head away. 'Yes,' the doctor said, covering her up. He turned with slight embarrassment to Mark. 'Could I have some soap?'

'Soap.' He went into the bathroom and brought back the slimy soap, left too long under somebody's flannel. The doctor was putting on a rubber finger-stall. Mark, in a cold rush of cowardice, began, 'I just have to go downstairs and—' but Charlotte said imperiously, 'Don't go away,' so he sat down on Georgina's bed again and took up a book, opening it and holding it like a shield.

'Just turn round,' the doctor said. 'That's right. Legs up a bit. This won't take a minute.' She screamed. Mark felt himself shaking, sweating, outraged with horror. She went on screaming, her hands clutching the pillow, her face buried. At last the doctor said, 'Yes,' and Mark raised his head. The child, assaulted, horrified, was pressed into the bed, her whole body shaking. The doctor said, 'Sorry about that, but it has to be done. Yes. Shall we talk outside for a moment?'

Mark followed him outside on to the cold landing. A movement upstairs made him look up, and he saw Georgina's face, pale and a little frightened, pressed against the banisters.

'Go and talk to her,' he said.

She ran down the stairs, grateful to be ordered to do what she wanted to do, and hurried into the bedroom, closing the door quietly.

'Well,' the doctor said, 'it's appendix. We'll have to get her off right away. Is there any particular hospital you'd like her to go to?'

Mark stared at him. 'No,' he said. 'No. But—how serious is it? How—?'

'Oh, it's not acute. Still, we'd better get her in. No knowing when these things are going to blow up.'

Mark said, 'I haven't the faintest idea what you're talking about. Will they operate?'

'Oh yes, I should think so.'

'But when?'

'I can't tell. Maybe tomorrow, maybe in a few days.'

'But tonight? Not tonight?'

'Possibly. It really depends on how they find her when she gets there.'

'But, good heavens, man, either she's got appendicitis or she hasn't—'

The doctor looked at him kindly and explained, as though making it entirely clear, 'It's only lukewarm at the moment. Better to operate when it's hot or cold. Now if I could use your phone I'll get on to the hospital.'

While he was telephoning, his soft voice seeming hesitantly to plead for a bed for Charlotte rather than demand one, Mark walked up and down the room, unable to keep still. The first hospital had no room. 'Try a nursing home,' he said furiously. 'The best one you know. Good God, I'll pay—' The doctor said, 'She would be much better in hospital,' and dialled another number. Again his gentle voice enquired, as though it were a matter of no particular consequence. This time he succeeded. He put the receiver down and said, 'The ambulance will be here in about half an hour.'

'Will I be able to go with her? That is, if Antonia isn't back?'

'Certainly.'

'But how will they know—I mean, who will see her? Will you be there?'

'No, no.' The doctor smiled again, winding his scarf round and round his neck, his eyes shining over it as over a yashmak. 'She'll be very well looked after. Don't worry.'

He plunged into the fog and, before he had reached the gate, was lost. Mark closed the door and stood helplessly facing the long misty hall, with its blotched and angry walls, one glove and a drift of old shopping lists for ever in the wooden bowl on the table. Georgina's cat Thomas came slithering along the wall, its tail erect and quivering. Suddenly Mark bent, took it by the scruff of its neck and threw it out of the house;

93

it leapt down the steps and disappeared. This small act of what Georgina and Antonia would have called cruelty made him more certain of himself. Now he would tell Charlotte. He brushed his hands, wet from the cat's fur, together, and went upstairs.

CHAPTER 9

MARK telephoned Georgina from the hospital. Through the glass door of the telephone booth he could see the visitors waiting in the hall, a dense, dark crowd carrying funereal flowers. The girl he had noticed as he came in was sitting on a hot-water pipe reading a book. He turned quickly as Georgina answered.

'Is Mummy home yet?'

'No, she isn't. Is Lottie all right?'

'She's just being looked at. Are you all right?'

'I can't find Thomas anywhere.'

'I expect he's out.'

'He wouldn't be out in the fog.'

'Well, if Mummy comes tell her there's no point in her coming down tonight. I'm just going to see Charlotte when she's in bed, then I'll be home.'

'You haven't seen Thomas?'

'No.'

'All right.'

They had told him to wait and then go up to Ward A with the visitors. They had wheeled Charlotte away down a tiled corridor. At first, at home, she had screamed; then, blanketed in red, carried on a stretcher to the lighted doorway of the ambulance, she had recovered her dignity, and after that she hadn't cried, even for him. Whatever they were doing to her he would never know, and he was more frightened and agitated than she was, attributing to her his own terror of loneliness and pain.

'What time are we allowed up?'

The girl looked at her watch—a cheap, heavy one on a leather strap—then at the clock on the wall. 'At seven. Four minutes to go.'

'I can't stand hospitals.' He clenched his fists inside his overcoat pockets, glaring down at the mosaic tiles between his feet.

'Have you been here before?' Her face was pale and rather pointed, with chopped black hair set anyhow on her head like a wig. He wondered whether she had had it all shaved off for an operation, then distractedly remembered that this was the fashion—his typists, too, were gnawed. The hair and face were planted in the upturned collar of a duffle coat below which was the part of her he had first noticed—the spindly tartan legs ending in square, crepe-soled shoes with the rubber peeling off at the toes. She was friendly, willing to talk to him.

'What?' he said. 'What? Oh—no. My daughter's just come in for an operation. Appendix.'

'How old is she?'

'Old? Eight. No. Nine yesterday. It was her birthday.'

'It's nothing, you know. It's not serious.'

'I suppose not.'

'I had mine out. I've still got the stitches in a tin.'

'You have?' He laughed quickly. She also laughed, showing small, pointed teeth like a baby's.

'Is she in the children's ward?'

'No. No, they didn't have a bed. She's in Ward A.'

'So's my mother. I'll show you where it is.'

'Thank you.'

He hadn't asked about her mother, but she told him, 'My mother's had everything out. You know, womb and so on. She says it makes her feel wonderful. I wouldn't have thought it was possible, but she says so.'

He looked at her, amazed. She stood up and, in spite of her legs under the square coat like a child's drawing, was small, almost breastless, with a long neck and long feet and long, unattended hands. She said, 'There. We can go up now.' The crowd was surging up the stairs, invading the quiet wards, bringing with it fog and germs and worry about the bills, sending up temperatures, scattering toffee paper; disturbing, alive, often unwanted. The girl said, 'I don't stay long. She likes me to come, but she doesn't like me to stay long. It's terribly difficult to think of anything to say, especially to one's mother.' She was trotting up the stairs beside him. He was hurrying, impatient to get there, as though he had not seen Charlotte for days, and he was out of breath, unable to answer her. She said, 'Of course it's different with a child. You can always play games or something.'

He nodded. The doors of the ward were open and he plunged in, looking from side to side for Charlotte, appalled by the rows of elderly women in bed. At last he saw her in a dark corner at the end of the ward. She was lying flat and smooth, only her head showing. He hurried up to her, asking nervously, 'Hullo, how are you? Everything all right? Feeling all right?'

'Where's Mummy?'

'She hasn't got back yet. How's the pain?'

'I want her.'

'She's been held up by the fog.' He sat down cautiously on the edge of the bed and took her hand. The thumbnail was painted scarlet and she tucked her thumb inside her fist, remembering it. 'There's a radio,' she said. 'Can you get it down for me?'

He unhooked the earphones and fixed them over her head. She frowned, concentrating on distant voices. He noticed the girl further along the ward; she waved, smiling at him, then turned to explain him to her mother, who stared and smiled and started rummaging in her locker. When he looked again the girl was walking down the ward, her crepe soles squeaking, holding a small paper bag. She came to the end of the bed and was held in Charlotte's grave look. She offered the paper bag awkwardly.

'Mother wondered if she was allowed sweets.'

'I don't know,' Mark said.

'I am,' Charlotte said. She took off the earphones and reached out for the bag. 'Is your mother here too?'

'Yes. That's her, in the green bed-jacket.' The little woman, who had been watching eagerly, waved again. Mark made a small, nervous gesture, feeling that everyone was staring at them. Charlotte said, 'Here come the doctors,' and clamped the earphones over her head again, making herself small in the bed. The girl walked away, with her hands in her pockets, and the doctors, as they passed her, looked at her briefly and smiled at each other, converging on Charlotte like assassins, paid for their work but not altogether unfeeling.

'Well, Mr Painton,' the sister said, taking away the earphones. 'I'm afraid you'll have to leave us.'

The doctors, young, undisciplined, stood at the foot of the bed talking among themselves. One of them glanced at Charlotte and, met by the petrified stare of her fantastic eyes, moved round and took her hand. Her eyes swivelled towards him, then back to Mark. His authority was destroyed. He could see that she knew he was powerless to help her, that he was going to abandon her. He wanted to ask them to be careful with her, but even this was beyond him. A nurse, holding a screen, was waiting for him to go. He kissed Charlotte, watched by the doctors, and turned quickly away. When he looked back it was all hidden from him.

He ran down the stairs, his hands clenched in his pockets, sickness souring his mouth. He had never asked himself why Charlotte meant more to him than all the others. He only knew that the thought of her body hurt or offended gave him physical agony. She was his only sensual pleasure, the only thing in his life whose beauty and delicacy had not been ravaged by habit. He had been reasonable and he would be reasonable again. As he stumbled and jumped down the stairs he felt only wild rage and disgust, a great horror that this was happening to her; a hatred, almost murderous, which extended beyond the doctors, with their clean hands and observing eyes, to include the whole of his small and now empty world, and beyond that again to the hostile, nightmare world which stretched to the horizons of his mind but of which he had no knowledge. At the bottom of the stairs he stood for a moment, his hands held out as though demanding where he could go, what he could do. The girl came quietly down behind him on her rubber soles, running sideways down the stairs, latching her coat as she ran. As she passed him she said, 'See you tomorrow.'

He watched her hurrying across the empty hall and the thought that she was on her way somewhere suddenly made him feel that if he was left alone he would go mad. He stepped forward and called out loudly, 'Just a minute—' She turned, surprised, her spindle legs caught in action, her head pivoting in the high collar. 'Me?'

'Yes.' Now that he had stopped her, he didn't know what to do. He walked forward towards her, trying to think. She relaxed, waiting for him.

'You—you're on your way somewhere, I suppose?'

'Yes. Why?'

'Nothing. I only thought—'

'I've got time for a drink, if you'd like one.' She looked at him enquiringly, as though ready to provide, within reason, anything else he needed.

'I can't, really. I—I'll make a phone call.' He knew

he was behaving absurdly and that her impression of him was so completely wide of the mark that he would never, in her presence, be able to resume his real self. In the mirror over the telephone he saw that his thinning hair was standing up on end and that his tie, a checked one bought by Georgina and worn only on occasional Saturdays, was crooked. The girl had sat down on the hot-water pipe again, her legs stuck out, heels on the floor, moving her feet in and out, toes together, toes apart. He watched her feet, as though they were two pendulums about to strike an hour. When, after some time, Georgina answered, he asked eagerly, 'Is Mummy back yet?'

'No.'

'Hasn't she phoned or anything?'

'No.' There was a pause, then, 'Are you coming back now?'

'Yes.' He remembered a hearty, cheerful tone which had once belonged to him. 'Look, you go and have your bath. Have a good hot one. I'll be back before you're out of it.'

'All right. The fire went out in the sitting-room, but I lit it again. I can't find Thomas.'

He thought of her kneeling by the grate, lighting the fire, with no one to see her, no one to be grateful. 'Are you all right, though?'

'Yes. Perhaps he went out, after all. You'll be coming home, then?'

'Right away.'

He came out of the phone box smoothing his hair. The girl stood up, and he realised that she was something else he had taken on, quite unnecessarily, and now had to get rid of.

'Well?' she asked. 'All right?'

'No. I'm afraid I haven't time.'

'Oh. . . .'

He fancied that she was disappointed, and yet did not see how this could be so. He had intruded himself, preventing her from hurrying away; now, without explanation, he was sending her on her way again. She shrugged slightly, and smiled. 'Oh well. . . .'

They walked together out of the hospital, and outside he glanced up at the great building, castellated and turreted like some dour castle, its windows bare, fog beating against its walls. The thought of what was going on in there, the vast loneliness in which its inhabitants slept and wept and died, again appalled him. If Charlotte was crying for him, he would never know, he would never have the idiot courage to find out. He almost leapt away down the street, the girl following closely behind him, her feet squarely slapping the wet pavement.

CHAPTER 10

WHEN Georgina put down the telephone receiver and all contact with the outside world was cut off she was on a ship at sea, alone, without radio or crew, without even the cat to keep her company. The fog beat and thundered against the large, uncurtained windows; the house, deserted, rocked on its course, abandoned to the ghosts and rats that were accumulating in its cellars, swarming its landings. She went back to the fire and knelt down, picking coal out of the scuttle and throwing it lump by lump on the yellow flames. A year, even a few months ago, such a fantasy would have comforted or at least occupied her. She clung to it desultorily for a little while, then let it go. The house was not a ship. The house was an empty house in the fog, in which, for the first time in her life, she was alone.

She was not going to have a bath yet, whatever he said. For one thing, it was too early; for another, the telephone might ring. The bathroom was a great distance away, isolated up the long stairs, and the fire might go out or someone come to the front door. A man, perhaps, who had seen them all go away. The idea of a man was more terrifying than a ghost. But then he would not ring at the front door. He would come noisily down the basement steps and break in through the bottom door. Or she would open the sitting-room door and see him standing there in the hall, waiting. She drew in her breath suddenly, her back rigid. Then she thought that when she opened the door and saw him standing under the light, waiting, he would be holding Thomas by the tail, dead. She could see him swinging the stiff body by its tail and coming towards her in boots. It was difficult to breathe, because there was no room left in her throat for breath, and her heart, which she had always thought securely fixed in the left side of her chest, shook her whole body.

She got up and turned round to face the room. Her face was pale, pink round the eyes and nostrils, her mouth drooping. She groped to plunge her hands in her pockets, but in the skirt which Antonia had made her put on there were none. Instead, she stuck her hands inside the waistband of her skirt and stood with elbows out, feet firmly apart, looking at the door. The thing to do, if the hall was empty, was to bolt the bottom door and the french windows in the dining-room so that anyone who might now be hiding in the fog could not get in. But if the hall was empty. When she took a breath it made a little noise, a sob. She walked forward, round the sofa, past the bookshelves, and put her hand on the cold metal doorknob. The latch was weak and could always be blown open by a gust of wind; before she had turned the handle the door had swung back a little on its squeaking hinges.

He was there. He stood under the light, in the fog that poured through the open front door. She saw nothing except the shape of him and the fact that his hands were empty. She slammed the door shut and ran away from it and then ran back, leaning against it, looking wildly round the room, pushing against the door with all her weight. There was no sound from the hall; no sound in the house, except for her own whimpering, which she hardly heard. She ran across the room and started pushing the reluctant, heavy sofa, her shoes skidding on the carpet. Before she had moved it more than a few inches there was a peremptory knock on the door and it swung wide open and the man was standing there, looking round angrily.

'Anyone at home except you?'

She didn't answer, crouched against the sofa. He slammed the door shut and walked heavily across the room to Mark's desk. She did not wait to see what he was going to do but darted round the side of the sofa, flung herself against the door, opened it, pelted down the hall, dived wildly into the fog.

When she found herself on the main road, a bright stream of which Sheldon Road was a dark tributary, she stopped running for a moment because she had no more breath. Even now, in the fog, there were plenty of people about. She looked up and down, wondering who she could ask for help. Noticing a child standing crying on the pavement without a coat, people wondered whether they should help her.

Neither they nor Georgina did anything about it; they hesitated, stared and passed on—Georgina because she was a child and her courage all spent, the passers-by because they thought somebody else would see to her and it was none of their business. Only the local eccentric, roaring his prophetic warnings and striding along in the gutter with his fez and sharp beard cleaning the fog, actually stopped, mounted the pavement and advanced on her as she stood in the bright light of a greengrocer's window. Seeing him, she jumped away from the light and ran on up the hill, remembering that somewhere up there was the police station where they had gone once to recover Antonia's handbag; and then she remembered that long before the police station, much nearer, just here past the church, was the road where Daniel lived. This, more than anything she could ever write in her diary, more than anything she could hope to do for years, would impress him. The thought was hardly conscious, but it was there. Strong with relief, she ran down the dark side road, looking for the number in the stained glass above the front door.

Daniel himself answered her insistent ring on the bell. She was too out of breath for a moment to say anything, and he stared at her as though he had never seen her before. In a thick brown dressing-gown and striped pyjamas he looked smaller, younger than he did at school, his hair standing up in short spikes over his scrubbed face. He asked blankly, 'What on earth do *you* want?'

'Oh, there's a man—' She felt she was going to cry again. 'There's a man—'

'You'd better come in.' He let her into the little hall and asked solemnly, without suspicion, 'What man?'

'In our house. They were all out. He just walked in through the front door. I suppose I couldn't have shut it properly after Daddy took Charlotte to the hospital—'

'You'd better tell my father.' He gave her a little shove, pushing her into the sitting-room. It was very small and warm, the television going with all the lights on and Daniel's father and mother sitting in fat cretonne armchairs on each side of a white-hot fire. His mother jumped up, spilling her knitting, saying, 'Good gracious, what's this? What's Georgina doing?' and his father looked up mildly, laying his newspaper across his knees. 'She says there's a man in their house,' Daniel said. 'Everyone else was out and she got away.'

In five minutes it was all explained. Mrs Greenbaum was horrified; she put her arms round Georgina and challenged over her head, 'Well, what are you going to do? Send for the police, send for the police!' Mr Greenbaum shook his head gently. 'The man will have gone by now. The thing to do is to ring up Georgina's father. If he is back, he will deal with it best.'

'But they can find the man!' Mrs Greenbaum insisted. 'Georgina knows what he looked like, don't you, pet?' Georgina nodded. Both she and Daniel turned from Mrs Greenbaum to Mr Greenbaum as they spoke. Sensing indecision and uncertainty, Georgina's throat again tightened with tears; she sat pinned down by the fat little hands, pressed against the taut skirt, tortured by the heat of the fire.

'You are not even sure,' Mr Greenbaum said, 'that he had any ill intent. Now are you, Georgina?'

'Ill intent! A man walking into an empty house like that! The child should never have been left alone. We know what might have happened.'

Georgina shivered. The heat of the fire was making her feel sick. She longed above all else for her parents, and particularly, with a sharp, almost painful need, for her mother. She said, 'I'm sure if you ring up somebody will be home by now. I'm sure they will.'

She could hear, as Mr Greenbaum waited, the sharp, endless ringing. Then Mr Greenbaum put the receiver down. 'Nobody there,' he said. For a moment no one spoke. Then Mrs Greenbaum began again, 'We must send for—' and broke off to wrap Georgina in her little arms, scooping her awkwardly on to her lap and blotting the child's tears on her solid satin breast.

In Sheldon Road the Paintons' house was deserted. The fog, sweeping in through the open door, drifted from room to room, climbed to the attics, shrouded the silent landings.

Next door, in a small top room, a woman turned to her husband and tried to reach for his hand.

'It was nice of them to let you phone. Will he be long?'

'Coming right away.' He turned desperately from her as the pain mounted again and he heard his voice in hers, crying for freedom.

CHAPTER 11

WHEN Mark saw Sangston's car parked under the street lamp he paid off his taxi and waited until it had driven away before going through the front gate. He closed the gate behind him and stood for a little while on the path, motionless, his hands in his pockets. He had taken the girl to a pub near the hospital, a noisy, garish place which normally he would have avoided. She had drunk one tomato juice, told him her name, which he couldn't remember; then, vaguely saying that she had to meet some people, she had gone, leaving him with an untasted whisky and an absurd, almost childish, feeling of resentment against her, himself and the world in general. To comfort himself, and also because he could not at first face the prospect of going home, he had drunk four more whiskies. Now, thoughtfully, standing in the fog, he was not considering anything, not wondering whether or not he was going to go in; he was merely paralysed for a few moments by reluctance at the prospect of climbing the steps, opening the front door, allowing himself to be swallowed up again. At last, slowly, with some unsteadiness, he walked up the steps, fell over the dolls' pram, found his key and fitted it into the lock. Almost immediately the door was flung open and he was taken off his guard, overpowered by Antonia's voice, her tears, her hands pulling him in.

'Where have you been? Where's Charlotte? Georgina was alone and a man came, she ran away, some awful man just walked into the house. Where have you been? Where's Charlotte?'

He blinked, looking down at her. He knew that Sangston had also come into the hall, but he did not look at him. 'Georgina?' he asked. 'Where is she? How do you know?'

'She went—oh, she went to the Greenbaums, they rang up, they'd been trying to ring up for hours. Where's Charlotte? Where's Charlotte?'

'In hospital. Having her appendix out.' Having said this, he walked deliberately along the hall, past Sangston, into the sitting-room and poured himself a drink. Meanwhile he heard, from some distance away, Antonia's voice. He saw her quite clearly and thought that she looked rather untidy. What she was saying was not, for the moment, important. When he had finished his whisky he interrupted her.

'Georgina's at the Greenbaums'. Is she all right?'

'You can hardly expect her to be all right after—'

'But not hurt?'

'She's got a slight temperature; they've put her to bed. Why didn't you take her down to the hospital with you? When are they operating? How serious is it?'

'Who was the man?' Mark asked. 'Does anyone know?'

'Of course not. Can I ring the hospital? Can I go down there?'

'Then how do you know there was a man at all?' he asked deliberately. 'How do you know she didn't make it all up? Just like Georgina.' He poured himself another drink and switched on the electric fire with his foot. 'Cold in here.'

Antonia was crying. Sangston put his hand on her arm. 'Is there anything I can do?'

'Why not go home?' Mark suggested amiably.

'Anything I can do, Antonia?'

She shook her head. 'Nothing at all,' Mark said. He felt a remarkable power, a feeling almost of contempt for both of them. He wanted to add kindly, 'And thank you for making love to my wife'; he was drunk enough to think that this would be devastating but not drunk enough actually to say it. When the front door had slammed, however, he said, 'I hope you had a pleasant day?'

'You're drunk, aren't you?'

'How you always say the right thing. Yes. A little.'

'Tell me which hospital she's at.'

For a moment, sly and jealous, he wanted to keep it from her. When he had told her and she was telephoning, his resentment against her sharpened almost unbearably. With a small madness he had never suspected he began questioning her right to interfere with Charlotte, to deprive him of his responsibility.

She put down the receiver with a little sigh of relief. 'Well, that's all right. She's fast asleep. They think they'll operate tomorrow, but it's not serious.'

'I know. Good God, I know. I took her down there.'

'I know you did. You sound as though I ought to thank you for taking her.'

'If, of course, you had been here you could have gone with her.'

'I know, but the fog—'

'Ah. The fog.'

'Well, you know how thick it was.'

'Oh yes, it was very thick. Still, I phoned at five, and you'd been gone for an hour. It's now'—he pulled out his watch, flicked it open—'midnight.'

'I was back here at ten. And found nobody here, no message, nothing. And the front door wide open.'

'I should hardly have thought it would take six hours to drive from Essex.'

'It didn't. We stopped for a meal on the way.'

'Oh. So it wasn't the fog at all?'

'No. Not altogether.'

'Then why did you say it was?'

She sat down in the wing chair, her hands clasped in her lap, her head bent. After a moment she looked up.

'Would you like something to eat?'

'No.'

She looked down again at her hands. There was a long silence. He then asked again, 'Why did you say it was the fog?'

'Mark, I don't know. Does it matter?'

'What are you so upset about, then?'

'It's Georgina. What might have happened. I can't stop thinking.'

He moved his shoulders irritably. The insistent presence of physical horror was too much for him. He snapped, 'But it didn't. You weren't thinking about Georgina when you stopped to have dinner with Sangston.'

'Of course not. I thought you—'

'Oh yes.' He walked quickly up the room and back again, trying to calm himself. 'Anyway,' he said, 'nothing did happen. She had a fright. Probably nothing to it.'

'To make her run away like that? In the fog, all alone?'

'You'll find out tomorrow.'

'It's tomorrow already.' She watched him pour another drink and stand with it in his hand, staring at the picture over the mantelpiece. The idea that she no longer loved him began, as she looked at him, to obsess her. It was as though a door she had thought permanently sealed, nailed up for comfort and protection against the outside world, had begun to swing open, not far enough for her to see what lay beyond but far enough to suggest the curious idea of escape. She said, 'This is the first time we've been alone. I mean, for years.'

'Yes.'

'I suppose if we had no children, this is what it would be like.'

'Possibly.'

'Why didn't you come straight home from the hospital? You knew Georgina was alone.'

'Because I didn't want to come home. I suppose that shocks you.'

'No,' she said quietly. 'I didn't want to come home either.' She got up, standing with her hands hanging loosely by her sides. 'But here we are.' She picked up her handbag and jacket, moving towards the door. He turned at last away from the picture and stretched his arms out along the mantelpiece, grasping it as though he would lift it. Then his arms slackened, dropped after the pointless effort. 'It's different for me.'

'Why?'

'I am a man.'

She said nothing.

'Well? You don't think so?'

Her back was towards him, her hand on the door. 'Of course I do, Mark.'

'You're lying.'

They waited, motionless, isolated together in the empty house. At last she said, 'This isn't real.'

'Real? Why isn't it real?'

'Because it doesn't make sense.'

'Why,' he asked despairingly, 'should it make sense?'

'You are,' she said cruelly, 'over forty. You're not young. Neither am I. This is a waste of time.'

'In the last five minutes you have said it all. Unreal. Not sensible. A waste of time. You know, don't you? You are absolutely certain? Did you think of this today, when you were having such a good time with Sangston?'

'What do you mean?'

'Or did you tell yourself the truth, that you are old, not so attractive any more, not so tempting?'

She opened the door. Her voice was steady as she asked, 'Have you seen Thomas? I ought to put him out.'

'No.'

'Don't say we haven't even got Thomas.'

'Antonia. Don't go.'

'You know, I have a feeling that my mother is ill. It's funny, I hadn't thought of it before.'

She closed the door quietly and walked along the hall, picking up more things on her way; a sandal of Charlotte's, a crayon, a hair ribbon; mounted the stairs more slowly than she had ever done before, the linoleum cold under her stockinged feet. What Mark had said must be true. She had seldom thought about herself before, had not anticipated any particular future, any change or finality. Her life had seemed to unravel smoothly from some inexhaustible source, and it was only now, surrounded by doors gaping on to empty rooms, that she realised that this was its furthest extent, that she was pulling against something that would give no more.

As the night passed the fog cleared, sinking back like a tide and at last seeping away even from the valleys and hollows of London. There were only two lights in Sheldon Road: the Paintons' sitting-room, shining behind thin curtains across gardens like derelict swimming pools, and the top room next door, a hard, square light which grew brighter as the fog cleared. The Army Officers' widows, responsibility never leaving them, slept harshly in their basements, their hair clamped in strong grey nets. The bed-sitting-rooms above them were mostly empty, the sober tenants scattered in the pursuit of love—mother's love, friend's love, love of a body, a voice in a week-end bed. Suspended, life waited to go forward, sluggish or springing violently from the dead hours.

CHAPTER 12

Antonia heard a bell ringing and, turning mutinously into the pillow, wondered why one of the children didn't answer it. It rang again, a mosquito buzz in the depths of the house. Still half asleep, she rolled out of bed, groped into her dressing-gown and was half-way down the stairs before she remembered there were no children and then, in a split second, every event of the day before. The sitting-room door was open, but the curtains were still drawn. There was no sign of Mark, no sign of life anywhere. When she opened the door she was dazzled by a cold blaze of sunlight.

The man standing on the doorstep looked bleached, broken with exhaustion. He said, 'I came to explain about last night. I couldn't leave until now.'

'Last night?'

'Well, I was afraid I startled your little girl. I shouldn't have done it in the normal way, but the front door being open I took the liberty. It's the first, you see, and I kind of lost my head with her screaming. So I thought this morning I'd better come and explain, just in case.'

'You mean it was you who came last night?' She felt she would have to put out a hand to prevent him from falling, but by some miracle he was keeping his balance, swaying towards her out of the sun. 'But what did you want?'

'To telephone.'

'Who? The doctor? Because your wife was having a baby?'

'That's right. I was afraid I startled your little girl.'

Her relief was so great that she laughed, clapping her hands to her mouth like a child. He smiled tentatively. 'I thought I'd better come and explain.'

'It's your first? A boy or a girl?'

'Boy,' he said. 'Whacking great baby, too—weighed ten pounds.'

'I'm so glad. Please don't worry about last night. You must be terribly happy.'

'I'm tired.'

'Well, I expect you are, but—'

'Can't stand operations, you know, that sort of thing. Oh well'—he grinned bleakly—'expect I'll be tired for the rest of my life now. You've got four. I've seen them playing in the street. Nice-looking kids. Just so long as it's all right about last night——'

'Perfectly all right,' she said. 'And if there's anything you want, if you want to telephone again——'

'Not till next year, thank you. So long.'

'Goodbye, and thank you.' She shut the door and called, 'Mark?' There was no answer, but she heard him coming out of the bathroom, walking across the landing. Picking up the skirts of her dressing-gown, she ran up the stairs and into the bedroom. He was tying his tie in front of the mirror. She sat down on the edge of the bed and plugged in the electric kettle.

'Who do you think that was?' she asked triumphantly.

'I don't know.'

'It was the man from next door. It was he who came last night, to use the telephone. Georgina couldn't have recognised him. Isn't it a relief.'

'I thought as much.' He turned away from the mirror. Freshly shaved, he looked old, more tired than he had done the night before. He scooped his change off the mantelpiece and dropped it into his pocket. 'How stupid,' he said. 'How unnecessary.'

'Aren't you glad?'

'Of course.'

'Everyone was a bit overwrought yesterday. I mean, things like that don't really happen, not if you stop to think. Everything's all right now, isn't it?'

'Yes,' he said. 'Everything is just the same.'

The lid of the kettle began jumping up and down; enveloped in steam, with great courage and skill, Antonia grasped the live thing and poured the water into the teapot. 'We'll go up and get her from the Greenbaums', shall we?'

'You go. I'm going out.'

'Out?' She looked up, startled. 'Where?'

'I'm going down to the hospital.'

'But they said not to go today. They said——'

'I'm going to the hospital.'

'But you won't be able to see her.'

She watched him walk across the room towards the door. Her relief killed, a curious feeling of fear took its place. 'When will you be back?'

'I don't know.'

'Goodbye, then.'

'Goodbye.'

She sat holding the teapot, listening as he ran down the stairs, opened the front door, slammed it behind him. Then she put the teapot down and hurried into the children's bedroom, holding back the curtain and looking out to see him striding across the road, hatless, coatless, his head bent as though the sunlight were driving against him.

When he was out of sight she let the curtain drop and stood looking at the unmade beds, the litter of books and toys. She saw Georgina's diary lying on the floor. She picked it up and read, 'Everything is back to normal, so I suppose what I wrote was only my imagination and anybody who reads this can jolly well TAKE CARE . . .' She tucked the diary under Georgina's pillow and ran into the bedroom, pulled on her clothes, did her hair, snatched up her handbag and raced downstairs. Only a few minutes after Mark had left she was hurrying up the street in the opposite direction.

'She is sleeping,' Mrs Greenbaum said. She wore, although it was nearly midday, a quilted dressing-gown and very small feathered mules. She stood back from the doorway, but even so there was no room to pass. Antonia, facing the shadowed hall, looked at her clearly; Mrs Greenbaum's little eyes were temporarily buried, burrowing down against the brightness of the sun. Antonia appeared like a shadow slanted across the crazy paving.

'But I must see her!' The urgency in her voice was not carried between them. By the time her words had reached Mrs Greenbaum they were flat, tentative, shy. She stepped inside the house. 'I am so grateful to you.'

'I am only glad she thought of coming to us,' Mrs. Greenbaum said emotionally. 'When you think of her all alone.'

'But, you know, it wasn't as bad as that. The man only wanted to use the telephone. He came round this morning and explained.'

'There! Would you believe it?' Mrs Greenbaum began to laugh. 'Won't that be a relief to her? There was the poor child imagining all sorts of things. Of course she's very highly strung—Daniel's just the same. But there, just wanted to use the telephone!'

'Yes,' Antonia said, 'that was all.'

'Well, you must come and tell her.' She led the way up the narrow stairs. Having laughed and climbed the stairs and spoken a good deal, she was soon out of breath. 'Even so,' she whispered, panting, 'just to walk into the house like that, frighten the poor pet . . .'

'Yes,' Antonia said. 'I'll dress her and then, if I may, phone for a taxi.'

'Why not leave her?'

'Oh, no.'

'Talk it over with her, then.'

The room was small, hot, dazzling with chintz. Georgina lay with her arms over the pink sheets and satin quilt, dressed in striped pyjamas, her face pale and sweating. 'The central heating,' Mrs Greenbaum whispered, 'keeps us nice and warm.'

Antonia nodded and sat down on the edge of the bed. She took Georgina's wet hand and said her name quietly. It was Mrs Greenbaum who wakened her, lowering her quilt bosom and stroking the wet hair back from the child's forehead and saying, 'Mummy's here, pet, Mummy's come to see you, you're all right, there, you're all right . . .'

Georgina opened her eyes and looked at Antonia. She moistened her lips and said, 'Oh, hullo. Can I have a drink?'

'Nice iced orange,' Mrs Greenbaum said, and at last went away.

'How are you?' Antonia asked. 'How are you, darling?'

'All right.' Then her eyes darkened. Her tongue went round her lips again and she asked, 'Where were you last night? What happened?'

'It was the fog. It took us hours to get home. But the man, darling—'

'Yes? Did you hear about it?'

'Of course. But it was only the man who lives next

123

door. His wife was having a baby. He wanted to telephone the doctor. That's all.' Again, almost desperately, she presented the amusing, the reassuring and ordinary truth. She smiled, anticipating Georgina's relief. 'That's all,' she repeated eagerly.

For a moment the child's face did not change. Then she turned her head to one side so that Antonia could only see the thin jaw-line, the hooded eye. 'How do you know?'

'He came this morning to explain. He said he was sorry he frightened you.'

'Did you tell him?' The dry lips were tight, the hand rigid.

'Well,' Antonia kept smiling, 'he knew. I mean, you left the house while he was telephoning. He knew.'

There was silence. The radiator creaked ominously, and Mrs Greenbaum, ice tinkling against the side of the glass she carried, came slowly up the stairs. 'So,' Antonia said, 'there's nothing to worry about.'

Georgina did not answer. She did not move until Mrs Greenbaum gave her the drink; then she raised herself carefully on one elbow, drank and fell back exhausted. 'It's the shock,' Mrs Greenbaum said. 'He should have told her he wanted to telephone. How was she to know what he wanted? Anybody would have been upset.'

Antonia let go of Georgina's hand and stood up. 'Yes,' she said. 'But he was worried about his wife, I suppose. Anyway, it's all over now.' She looked round the room. 'Where are your clothes?'

'I'm not going home?' For the first time Georgina's voice was sharp. She looked anxiously at Mrs Greenbaum. 'But I've got a temperature!'

'We'll take a taxi.'

'But I don't feel well!'

'You can't stay here,' Antonia said, turning with a vest in her hand.

'Why not?'

'Because— Of course you can't.'

'But why not?'

'We would like to keep her,' Mrs Greenbaum said with unexpected firmness, 'if you will let her stay.'

'But—' Deprived, bewildered, Antonia hesitated. She held out the vest and took a step forward. 'No. You must come home.'

Georgina turned her head quickly, shutting her eyes. Mrs Greenbaum went out, leaving the door ajar. 'It's ridiculous,' Antonia pleaded. 'You can't stay here, for no reason.'

'I've got a temperature,' Georgina muttered savagely. 'It's nearly a hundred.'

'That's not very much.'

'It's gone up. I can feel it.'

Again Antonia sat down on the edge of the bed. She pulled at a knot in the vest's ribbon, and when it was undone, smoothed straight, she asked casually, 'Why don't you want to come home?'

'I do want to come home! I do! I do!' Wildly, as though maddened by stupidity, Georgina beat the bedclothes with her clenched fists. 'It's just that I don't want to come *now*!'

Antonia stood up and pulled back the curtain a little way. Below her, concentrated, deft, unhurried, Mr Greenbaum was cleaning his car. She let the curtain fall and said in a flat voice, 'Very well. You can stay for today.'

'For tonight?'

'Yes.'

There was a moment's silence, and then Georgina said, 'It makes a change. That's all.'

'Change?' The pale, bony face was very like Mark's; the tone of voice, casual and urgent, was Mark's. 'What do you mean?'

'Nothing. Is Thomas back?'

'No,' Antonia said bitterly. 'I haven't seen him.' She folded the vest again and put it back on the chair. 'Well, I must go.'

'But there's nobody there, is there?'

'Still, there's a lot to do. There's always a lot to do. The house is such a mess.' She laughed nervously. 'It looks as though a bomb's dropped. It's a good thing you're all away, really; perhaps I can clean your room for once. . . .' She stopped, seeing Georgina looking at her steadily, without pity. 'Charlotte's having her operation today.'

'Is she?'

'Don't you care?'

'Well, she isn't going to die, is she?'

Five minutes later Antonia walked quickly up the hill between the neat stuccoed houses—ugly and neat houses, like prison cells, with women staring out from behind polished windows while men laboured outside on their cars and gardens. She knew, now, that she was not going home. She had not chosen freedom—she could no longer escape it. What she had said to Georgina about the house was the last deception of herself. Alone, she faced the day with fear, as though it were an unknown land.

CHAPTER 13

'No,' Mark said. 'They won't let me see her. I didn't have to come.'

'Then why did you?'

He avoided the question, holding open the door for her. Bending a little, she stepped underneath his arm and waited for him. He looked up at the hundred windows, the towers. 'You would think,' he said, 'that even if she was asleep one could see her.'

'But there wouldn't be much point.'

'No.' He smiled, because her voice was gentle. 'Shall we walk a little? It's a wonderful day.'

'If you like.'

She walked in the sun with her collar up, her hands in her pockets, as she had done last night in the fog. She wore, as far as he could tell, no make-up, her mouth pale and dry as a child's, her eyes fixed brooding on the toes of her shoes. After a few minutes he asked, 'How's your mother?' A muscle under his left eye had begun to twitch violently, and as he waited for her answer he covered it with his hand so that he did not see her any longer, only the endless, shimmering street.

'Happy.'

'Do you live with her?'

'No.' She stopped suddenly, planted on the pavement. 'Where are we going?'

He uncovered his eye, but did not look at her directly. 'I don't know. I expect you're on your way somewhere.'

'I'm meeting some people.'

'Yes, of course.' How absurd of him to assume that she also did not know what to do, where to go. She knew exactly, whereas he, after this one definite gesture of coming down to the hospital when there was no need, was completely at a loss. He felt his cheek, looking away from her.

'I'm sorry,' he said, although he was not sorry; rather irritated by her self-sufficiency, blaming her for leaving him alone. 'How do you go?'

She shrugged, tracing a crack in the pavement with the toe of her shoe. 'Tube.'

'But we're coming away from it!' Savagely, he wanted to make her realise how unreasonable and childish she was being. 'The station is back there.' He pointed back down the long street. 'Past the hospital,' he insisted.

She smiled. 'It doesn't matter. There's another one up here.'

'Oh well, then, in that case—' He started off again, walking more quickly, as though it were he who had the appointment to keep. Selfish, he said to himself; bloody selfish. Lack of sleep and some greater, deeper lack, the feeling of having no identity, of being in some way invisible and intangible to the ordinary world, made him unable to judge the situation. The girl might have been a close friend who, at some crisis in his life, was letting him down. He forgot that he had not admitted to himself, let alone her, that he had come to the hospital to see her; that he had known they would not allow him to see Charlotte. He blamed her in his mind for letting him come, even dragging him all this way for nothing. At the end of the street, whichever direction she took he would take the opposite. Unless—and the thought brought him to an abrupt standstill—unless he followed her.

'I'm sorry. I'm not well.'

'Not well?' Her voice, slightly alarmed, came from behind him.

'No. I'd better go. . . .' He looked helplessly up and down the street, which now had no beginning and no end. 'I'd better go. . . .'

'Is anything wrong? Are you ill?'

Again he was irritated by her lack of understanding. Why, he demanded, couldn't she see what was the matter without being told? Why must she question him all the time? Why, if she was going, didn't she do so? 'Worry,' he said. 'Very little sleep and so on. That's all. Run along.'

'But you may not be all right.'

'No,' he snapped. 'I may not be.'

'Then what—but what—do you want me to do?'

'Nothing.' In order to avoid walking on, but because he must obviously go, he plunged out into the street, crossing it diagonally, while she ran behind him with little jumping steps, her hands still in her pockets, her head, trying to keep track of him, on one side.

'Look,' she said, 'I can't just leave you.'

He stepped up on to the pavement. The diversion had been useless, for he still had to decide which way he would go.

'Will you go home?' she asked.

'No.'

'Why not? Surely—'

Her stupidity enraged him. He could see himself trapped in this street for the rest of the day, running from side to side of it while she followed, plaintively questioning. 'My wife,' he said, 'has gone.'

'Gone? Gone where?'

'I don't know. Away.'

The girl's face became calm, as though a blind had been drawn down at a death. At last, he realised, he had said something she could understand. 'So you have nowhere to go?'

'Well, not exactly—that is, not exactly—'

'You'd better come with me.' It was not an invitation but a resigned acceptance. She was like a doctor who has been excited and distressed by strange symptoms which turn out to be nothing more than a common cold. She would cure him, but without joy. She turned back up the street. 'Come along.'

He followed her because, after all that, it would have been difficult, almost impossible, for him to refuse. At the same time the puny victory filled him with dismay. When she flung over her shoulder, 'I should think you've got a hangover, I should think that's it,' he did not answer. Her thin, trousered legs stalked haughtily along, the top of her head—all that could be seen—bounced up and down, her elbows were tucked neatly to her sides. Whereas before his distracted thought had been that he would follow her, it was now that he would stand still and let her march on alone; she would certainly never turn back to look for him. Curiosity, however, and the feeling that so long as he was with her he did to some extent exist made him keep on her track. At least she was going somewhere; and once they had reached their destination, wherever that was, he would be free to leave. She need never discover the lie about Antonia. Anyway, it was not wholly a lie; it was, looked at in one way, the truth. By going away, he argued, rubbing his eye, breathing heavily at the unaccustomed speed, he had meant exactly what had happened, and if the girl had misunderstood him it was her fault. From such close proximity that they could hardly see each other, he and Antonia had been torn apart, lost each other. He was no longer sure what she would at this moment be doing.

'We shall have to hurry,' the girl said, wheeling right and starting down a new street. He ran a few steps to catch up with her.

'Are your'—he panted—'are your friends very particular?'

'Particular?'

'Mind you being late?'

'No. But I'm never late. I don't believe in it. Do you?'

'I don't know. I suppose I am never'—he swerved

round her, walking on the outside so that she was trapped between him and the padlocked shops—'never deliberately late. But women—'

She smiled, and he did not finish the sentence. She made him feel that she was as far in advance of him as a grown-up with a child struggling to express itself; impatient, but tolerant of ideas she had long since discarded. He wished he could finish the sentence unexpectedly, startle her, but knew that nothing in his experience would do this, nothing even that he could invent. Like Georgina saying she had seen twenty-four dead rats or the Queen in a bus queue, the wildest effort of his imagination would be frustrated by a contemptuous, adult smile. He could think of nothing that would impress her. He said, 'My name is Mark Painton. I forget whether I told you.'

'Yes,' she said. 'You did. Last night.'

'I see.' He thought of this as meaning that he had told her a lot of things last night that he had now forgotten. He asked hesitantly, 'You told me yours?'

'I did.'

He laughed, covering his eye. 'But I've forgotten it.'

For a moment he thought that she was going to say tartly that if he had forgotten it she would not tell it to him again. To his great relief she also laughed, turning to him before she stepped into the echoing hall of the tube station, beckoning him on in the feeble yellow light. 'Barbara,' she said. 'That's not hard to remember.'

'Let me—' He held out a florin. She took it, bought the tickets and gave him the change. 'It's funny that I don't remember. I was thinking it was something like Ann, Annette, Anna. . . .'

'No,' she said. 'Barbara.'

'And yet I could have sworn—' He stood behind her in the lift, not because it was full but because she stood ready to leave at the gates and looked with interest at the advertisements for brassieres and corsets that embarrassed him, were his secret thoughts displayed in public so that he recognised them without ever having looked at them squarely, the pointed breasts and attenuated legs for ever, thank God, inaccessible. It both shocked and disturbed him that the girl was so blatantly concerned with her body, must presumably see some similarity between herself and the drawings on the posters. He wished that he could distract her attention, but could not even remind her that he was there. He was becoming obsessed with the need to impress himself on her, to see the mould of himself on some other person. With no means of seeing his reflection, deprived of all his familiar mirrors, he was becoming less and less certain of his own reality. He longed for someone to call him by name.

'Mark.' She was outside the gates, the subterranean tunnel curving away behind her. 'Mark. Are you all right?' He stepped quickly out of the lift and again followed her.

CHAPTER 14

ANTONIA, abandoned on the northern hill of London, still believed that soon, that at any moment, she would have to go back. Her morning, with its unexpected freedom, was part of the impermanence of Sunday: the sunlight would not last; the empty streets, the distant clamour of bells, the freshness of the undisturbed air was no more than a mirage. Lovers, as the day passed, would feel a particular sadness; those who were lonely, knowing it would soon be over, grow hopeful. Little by little God withdrew and by nightfall would be gone, candles pinched, doors bolted, the last echo dead. Men left their overcoats at home and tortoises crept out of the leaves, but not for long. To Antonia the day was a dream which would instantly disappear, leaving no trace.

She was so certain of this that she began almost guiltily to enjoy herself. She felt at first the freedom of a child left for a little while without its parents: that she could do what she liked, although she did not know exactly what that was; that she could go or stay, although she did not know where; that she could behave, walk, speak in an exceptional manner, one that would not be recognised by her family: limp, smile at her reflection in a shop window, tell lies about herself and be believed. She was surprised to find how easily she was allowed on a bus, how indifferently the conductor took her money; surprised that no one seemed to speculate why she was on the loose, free to travel about at this time on a Sunday morning un-attached and with no apparent purpose. The bus hurtled past the entrance to Sheldon Road, and she looked back curiously, as though to see whether it had changed during her absence.

Even so, it did not occur to her to go very far away. When the bus stopped at the entrance to the park she got out obediently, for this was the perimeter of her world and to go beyond it did not yet seem necessary. As though walking behind the children, she looked carefully to left and right before crossing the road and turned away from the playground towards the lake, as though saying what she had so often said: the sand is not clean and, after all, do be reasonable—we have our own swing in the garden. When she sat down at first, automatically, she began to worry, her eyes searching about, her body tense, ready at any moment to jump to a rescue. Hardly noticing the sun, she unbuttoned her coat, pulled off her gloves, narrowed her eyes to watch the boats skimming and flying on the lake. They turned, plotted their courses, as though the patch of water were an ocean. Rowing-boats creaked laboriously from shore to shore, girls leaning back against the damp cushions imagining themselves queens, young men imagining nothing, struggling with the slimy oars. On the bank children stood watching, dangled jam jars, were snatched from drowning and led away with desolate howls. After a time Antonia barely glanced at them. She began to pity the women who, hardly daring to blink their eyes, were dragged about like protesting kites, the men who walked quickly as though under arrest, staring about them hungrily but clamped to sticky or warmly mittened hands. For the first time she was conscious of looking at her own world from the outside, and in the straggling procession along the water's edge recognised herself, her children, even Mark; and then bit her lip; and then openly smiled, for they suddenly appeared as absurd as the intent and tragic faces of clowns.

The extent of her freedom now seemed greater than it had before. She began to feel restless, to wonder how she could make the best of it. It was foolish simply to sit on a bench in the sun, although this was what she had often dreamed of doing. Most of the things she had often dreamed of doing now seemed insufficient and pointless. She did not, she realised, want to rest; she did not want to be alone. She got up and walked along the path towards the bridge. Already the air was colder, the water ruffling against the banks. People were leaving the park, and she supposed that this was because on Sunday they had lunch late; she had heard that this was so. This was the first Sunday for many years that she had not been getting lunch early, so that Mark could take the children out; even in summer, when the sun would last and her dress clung to her back and thighs as she counted a just number of roast potatoes on to hot willow pattern plates, she remembered herself presiding over an endless succession of such rituals, all based on some obscure kind of fear: that if the children didn't go out they would get, perhaps, diseases; that if Mark were not with them for an exact time it would lead to a weakening in some way of love. She had been so obedient. What, now, could she obey? The time of day, lunch time? The day of the week, Sunday? She was neither hungry nor, alone, religious. The reliable authority in herself which might have told her to go home, order, organise, was gone. There was no one she could go and see; no one who would not be outraged at meeting her without Mark or a child; no one, without Mark or a child to act as a bridge over the always immense gulf, whom she wanted to see.

She told herself that she would walk once more round the lake; she was growing colder, walking more quickly. She began to think, always keeping the obvious one back, of her friends and realised that without Mark they were less to her than strangers. She did not know, with only one exception, anybody. She was lonely, and recognising this, naming it, she realised that she had often been lonely, that in fact her life had been solitary, remote, spent in deep contemplation of the stomachs and temperatures of children, in a state of unvaried love which had stunted, if not entirely destroyed, feeling. Supposing in fact she was incapable of anything else; supposing the answer was that she was, away from her reflections, nothing; that she herself was no more than a reflection, possessing no separate heart? As she walked she looked into the faces of the people who came to meet her and then passed by: not one showed any sign of having seen her. They looked towards her, beyond her; no look was arrested by her face, no head turned, not even a child gave her a cursory stare. They walked, as it were, through her towards their definite destinations. She left the park suddenly, hurrying and without looking back, running across the road without thinking first of safety.

The telephone box, when she had closed the door, was warm, even comfortable; it was really all one person would need to protect them from the weather, to carry on every function of life. She leant against the glass, putting her handbag on the rack provided, glancing at herself in the mirror provided, noticing a drawing scratched on the wall, which, since it was Sunday, had not been removed by whoever the expert and invisible officials are who come with india-rubbers in the night. Even though she was alone, the drawing embarrassed her; she could have looked straight at it, but she looked away, turning her back on it as she ran her finger up the Sanitary Inspectors, Window Cleaners and Appliances, prodding the book with her round, unvarnished finger-nail while reaching with her free hand for the receiver and the three pennies she had put ready. But then, when it was all done and the number ringing, she made herself, or allowed herself, to look again and was astonished that there was anybody who connected such a thing with pleasure; and yet at the same time felt something

139

like envy, wonder that in anyone's dreams there could exist an image of such fabulous potency. Do people wish for this, she wondered; men? Do I myself?

'Antonia.'

She was so surprised to hear herself named that she half turned, flushed with embarrassment. 'How did you know?'

'I was expecting you to ring.'

'Oh. Well.' She laughed nervously, her back turned completely to the wall. 'Why?'

'How are things going?'

'Things? You mean Georgina and Charlotte? They're all right.' The mouthpiece was damp; she tried not to breathe into it. 'David, I—'

He interrupted her. 'You mean Georgina is all right? You've seen her?'

'Yes. This morning. She doesn't want to come home. She's staying there for today.' She laughed again: how absurd of the child, a whim of course. She heard the laugh and found it foolish, exasperating. It was not funny. How could she break out? How say what she meant, strike the true word, the real feeling? 'David, I—'

'And so you are on your own? Apart, of course, from Mark.'

'Mark is away too.'

'Away?' The voice snapped, instantly suspicious. 'What do you mean—away?'

'I mean—' She hesitated, forced herself to speak. 'He's gone.'

There was a short silence. He was not, apparently, able to understand. She could hear his breathing, she could hear him thinking, quick, sharp thoughts, a rapid calculation of thoughts. He did not then say what she expected him to say. He asked stiffly, 'And so?'

'Well . . .' It was impossible not to laugh again: and so nothing, it is simply a fact, a piece of news of no importance; I don't want anything from you. But again she forced herself to the almost impossible hurdle. 'I thought I might come and see you.'

There was another silence. 'We are going to lunch with my sister.'

'Oh well, in that case—' she began quickly, so anxious to be released, so hurt, the laugh again blurring the edge of her voice. 'Naturally—'

'You could come too.'

'Oh no—'

'Can you come round? I'm not dressed.'

She tidied her temporary home before she left, replacing the telephone book, untangling the flex, removing her handbag. She glanced at the mirror, touching her hair, but did not again look at the drawing. She stepped out into the street like a woman who has set everything in order, shutting the door carefully behind her. She was trembling, but possibly this was from hunger, the uncommon lack of sleep.

CHAPTER 15

WHEN the girl pushed open the door, impatiently waiting for Mark to follow, the first person he saw was Teasdown: Teasdown monumental, inevitable, turned towards the door as though placed there by fate; Teasdown floating in a blue haze, a pint glass of beer in his hand. At first Mark forgot the girl and stood where he was, his head stretched forward, staring incredulously at the huge, sad face; then he remembered the girl too sharply and stepped back, colliding with a young man nursing a dachshund, who said shrilly, 'Oh! How clumsy!' The young man quivered, singling Mark out; the dachshund looked out of his arms with shining, loving eyes, being protected.

Mark snapped, 'I'm sorry,' and turned quickly back to the bar, where the girl was waiting, tapping her fingers on the brass rail. The little room was packed tight; those who had got there at midday sat with their knees swivelled sideways, their glasses held under their chins, inaccessible sandwiches on tables which had been pushed farther and farther away; those who had come late could move only their heads and snatch every rare opportunity for drinking, bending to glasses which could not be raised to their lips. Mark could not see how it was possible for the girl to meet anyone here; and then, to his dismay, he saw wherever she looked heads nodded in welcome; that Teasdown himself had managed to raise a hand. She had come to meet all of them.

This was the time for him to go, if he could. He turned and again met the dachshund's bright gaze. It yapped smugly, drawing attention to itself; the young man drew it closer, looking fiercely at Mark. The girl, having reached her destination and been acknowledged, was still waiting. Recognition grew slowly over Teasdown's face and at last broke. 'Painton!' he shouted. 'Well, dear boy!' Like someone recognised while wearing fancy dress, Mark smiled foolishly, gave a feeble wave. Another influx pushed him forward, and he found himself standing by the girl, still smiling, over her head at Teasdown. 'Well,' he said, 'we meet in—' But Teasdown was talking to someone else, he did not hear. Again Mark felt a contraction, a diminishing of belief in himself. Having seen someone who actually knew him, a witness to his existence, it was alarming when the witness apparently deliberately refused to give evidence. Worried, keeping watch on the broad, familiar back, Mark asked, 'What will you drink?'

She again drank tomato juice. She seemed in no hurry to meet any more closely the people she had come all this way to see. She said in a resigned, business-like voice, 'Tell me about your wife.'

He hardly heard her, humbly and anxiously staring

143

at Teasdown. 'Do you know that man? The fat one. The tall one.'

She turned her head in the great coif of her collar. 'Yes. He's a Q.C. His wife keeps a hat shop. Why?'

'Funny thing. I met him yesterday in Madam Tussaud's.'

'You must lead a very odd life.'

'Me? Odd?'

'Yes. Going to Madam Tussaud's.'

'Oh, I take the children . . .' Teasdown had turned his head, and Mark smiled eagerly.

'How's hell?' Teasdown called.

'What?' Mark said. 'What?' He could not believe that this was what Teasdown had said, but was prepared and anxious to answer. Then to his astonishment the girl smiled.

'Fine,' she shouted. 'Red and rocky.'

'Three dimensional, I hope.'

'No. Vistavision.'

'I'm sure you should know, dear.'

'We were thinking of coming to you for a first-hand opinion!'

'Bitch. . . .' Apparently much pleased, beaming as Mark had seen him at some obscure judicial wit, Teasdown again turned away. The girl, too, had been entertained. Her smile seemed too big for the small face, stretching it from ear to ear, baring the sharp milk teeth. 'You see,' she explained kindly, 'we are working on hell for this Faust story—'

Mark brought his hand down flat on the counter with such force that the palm stung. For a moment he felt throttled, unable to follow up the violent gesture with words. A few people turned to look at him with interest. 'I don't understand.'

'It's quite simple,' she said coldly. 'The art department in designing hell. I work in the art department. Films. You know?'

'Ah,' he said. 'Films.' What did she think of him? Rip van Winkle? Did she think he didn't understand films, know from Georgina, even know someone who worked making them? But he kept this back, feeling it might be a trump card. He was dismayed by the need he felt for physical action, as though the more confused and uncertain he became the more his body must insist, prove his reality. Feeling the insufficiency of 'Ah. Films', the imbecility of pretending to know, he suddenly grasped her arm above the elbow, his fingers pressing through the thick, hard sleeve. 'Where are these people you came to meet?'

With her free hand she pulled his away, not roughly but as though returning it to him. 'Do you want to meet people?'

'Certainly. Certainly, since I've come all this way.' He looked round, challenging. The dachshund again whimpered, and the young man said, 'Barbara, darling couldn't you ask your friend to keep his elbow out of Putzi's eye?'

'My elbow wasn't in his eye.'

'Oh, but it was. You keep jogging her.' He turned the dog over on its back, nursing it like a baby; its eyes shone malevolently at the far end of a stomachful of greyish nipples, its short legs sagged open, repulsively abandoned.

'Ridiculous to bring a dog here,' Mark said, 'to a place like this.'

'Ridiculous?' The young man turned his head from side to side as though suddenly wound up. 'Did you say ridiculous?'

'Bloody silly, getting in everyone's way.'

'Do you know this man? Barbara, do you know this man?'

'Yapping,' Mark shouted incoherently. 'Making a nuisance of itself!'

'Is he insane?' the young man asked. 'Is he mad?' His arm curved protectively as he hitched the dog higher; above the fragile, pointed face of his love, his child, his own face trembled with indignation and fear. 'Someone take him away,' he screamed softly. 'Someone tell him to go.'

When the girl asked Mark afterwards what he had really intended to do, he said he didn't know, that he had intended nothing. This was not true, because not only did he want more than anything else in the world to tear the dog out of the loving arms: he intended to do so. This was his plan, visualised in every detail: the wrenching of the dog away, the throwing of it, a soft and living weight, as far as his strength could throw it; the feeling of it at one moment in his hands—at the next, gone. This was all, a desire so intense that relief had come almost before he stretched out and closed his fingers round the dog's body and pulled it away. For a horrible moment he held it, squirming. Then he felt a sharp pain in his face, the dog dropping out of his hands, pain extraordinarily resulting from the hands tearing at his face; and kicks, sharp kicks, at his legs and body; a wide-open mouth so close to his that he could see the pale, ridged palate.

Curiously, in the brief moments that he was released from the young man's fury, he thought of Edward. Before trying to cover his face again, to ward off the undirected blows, he could see the child as clearly as in the lens of a camera; then the business of protecting himself absorbed him again until the next lull, when, astonished, he found himself wondering whether he would ever be able to afford Harrow. It was as though his mind, having allowed a moment of phenomenal release, had slammed shut, trapping only one thought. He saw his hand raised in front of his face and that there was blood on it. He did not think he was fighting back; he had no wish to do so.

The attack was finishing. It was not yet over, but others were moving in, arms fell like barriers between them. Mark found himself thrown back against Teasdown, sprawled against him, off his balance. Only a few yards away the young man, the dachshund gathered into his arms, was weeping with high, regular screams, like a newborn child. At first Mark could not see the girl. He looked round desperately, but she seemed to have gone. Then her voice came from behind him. She was holding Teasdown, supporting him after the impact of Mark's fall.

'He isn't well,' she said. 'He told me so. His wife's left him.'

'No!' Mark said.

'You'd better go home,' Teasdown said.

'No!'

'You'd better go before we call the police.'

He turned swiftly towards this new menace. 'The police?'

The thick woman in tweeds, her face crimson over a spotted bow tie, poked her head at him; he felt a spray of spittle on his cheek, but could not raise his arm to wipe it away.

'Brute! Beast!'

'Now then, Molly,' Teasdown said.

'If I could get my hands on you—' She would murder him, Mark knew; her little purple hands would exultantly murder him for his assault on the dog. Looking round the room, he realised with the first shock of fear that he had become an object of intense hate. To be hated so much, on such grounds, made him angry. The fear and the anger, unlike his desire to destroy the dog, gave him no pleasure. He only wanted to escape, to be safe. But when he tried to move they, and the buttress of Teasdown behind him, moved too. Someone said, 'At least you should apologise to Bobby.'

'I do. But I do.' Fear was uppermost now; any ruse to find a way out. He said to the inconsolable young man, 'I am really desperately sorry. I am really sorry.'

'You don't know how much she means to me.' The little crowd round him nodded, murmured, leaned lovingly towards him. Mark said roughly, 'I do know.'

He was now feeling sick with the warm blood in his nose, the taste of it in his mouth.

'She is like a child to me,' the young man said. 'You are a monster.'

'Yes,' said Mark. All this he already knew. It was not getting them anywhere. Perhaps he should go down on his knees before the bitch and beg its forgiveness. Then they would really think he was mad. Then he would really be mad.

He was more frightened now than he had ever been since he was a child, since the glistening eyes of the fox fur had watched him from every shadow. He was not what they thought him. They were not seeing him, Mark Painton, but, as they said, some monster, brute, beast, lunatic. It was fantastic. Every face was a mirror reflecting a strange and horrifying image, himself; nowhere could he see reflected the sober and loving man, husband, father, that he knew himself to be. 'I am not—' he began, 'I did not—' As he spoke he saw an extraordinary thing: in the misty, mildewed mirror behind the bar a face began to move, its mouth to open. He stared. The face stared back at him, bloody, wild, alarmed. Behind it, as in some crude representation of Good and Evil, Teasdown's great pale face hovered with an expression of stern benevolence. This hurts me, he seemed to be saying, more than it hurts you. Mark raised his hand to his mouth, stared at it smeared with dried and brownish blood. The man in the mirror looked up from his hand. A woman laughed a short bark of laughter that cut through the silence, splintered the image. Lowering his head, Mark blundered towards the door, through the door, out into the air. He began running and hurrying along the street, unable to keep up an even pace, stopping once or twice and then plunging forward, meandering from side to side of the empty afternoon pavement. Behind him, unnoticed, silently on her rubber soles, the girl followed.

CHAPTER 16

'I MUST go home.'
   'Why not telephone?'
   'No. I must go home.'
'But if she isn't there?'
'She will be.'
'But I thought you said—'
'She will be there!' Mark shouted. The girl had
caught up with him while he was calling for a taxi.
Now the taxi driver waited, indifferently lighting a
cigarette while the disordered, bleeding man argued
with the girl on the kerb. Chelsea types. He dismissed
them with the match thrown into the gutter, sighed,
waited. Gulls soared and circled high in the thin air.
In the sunlit, drugged Sunday afternoon only the gulls
and the quarrelling couple were alive and raucous.
'In any case,' Mark said, his hand on the door, 'even
if she isn't, I must go home.'
   'Not like that. You don't know what you look
like.'
   'I am going home.'
   The man was in. The girl would follow, of course;
probably a bit of a fight over the door, first—him
trying to keep it shut, her trying to open it. Patiently,

not even bothering to take off the brake or put down his flag, the taxi driver waited.

'I'm coming with you.'

'Why?'

'You said she'd gone, didn't you?'

'I said—' The door slammed. Without turning or taking the cigarette out of his mouth, the driver put down his flag and asked, 'Where to?', then closed the dividing window. He had no wish to overhear their conversation. Natter, natter, he knew how it would be. The only thing to watch out for was if one of them jumped out, the one with the money for the fare. Probably the girl. Chelsea types.

Mark leant back, closing his eyes, holding his handkerchief to his face. He was shut now, imprisoned in himself, a willing victim to his own disgust. By covering his face and closing his eyes he could hide from the outside world, from the persecuting, inescapable girl. His body was jolted and shaken, as though bones, nerves, muscles had been thrown carelessly into the sack of his skin; his throat dry and constricted, as though here the sack had been drawn tight, leaving his head lolling from side to side. He only wanted to think of his own beastliness, to convince himself of it, to avoid the smallest distraction. By the time he got home, if he could concentrate strongly behind closed lids, he might feel a shock of horror and then, blessedly, shame. He longed to hear himself saying, 'I don't know what came over me. There was this dog . . .' and to see Antonia's eyes soften, her hands and body move into the rites of forgiveness. He did not doubt for a moment that she would be there and willing to listen to him. He would take her attention away from Georgina and fasten it for once on himself. The sight of him would be enough. Where have you been, what have you done, what has happened? At last there would be an answer to all those questions, and, if he could manage it, he would be ashamed.

The damned girl was in the way. He was conscious of her sitting beside him and of her silence. To get rid of her he would have to admit that he had lied. That didn't matter: a liar as well as everything else, but only for as long as it took him to get home. He said roughly, 'It wasn't true what I said about Antonia. She'll be there.'

After a slight pause she asked composedly, 'How do you know?'

'Because, of course, she will. She never left. Nothing of the sort. You'd better get out.'

'I'll see you home.'

'You think I'll do something else?' he asked curiously. 'What?'

'How do I know?' She shrugged her shoulders, pressing her feet against the opposite wall of the taxi and, as usual, inspecting them as though they were strange to her, unexpected phenomena. 'After that, anything.'

He was tempted too far. 'How did it seem?' he asked. 'What happened?'

Again she shrugged her shoulders. 'There seemed no reason for it. Just a little dog like that.'

'It seemed mad to you?' he insisted. 'You thought,

they all thought, I didn't know what I was doing?'

'Well,' she asked, 'did you? What did you mean to do?'

He leant back again, muffling his face. 'Nothing. I don't know.' And then, without looking at her, 'Why don't you leave me alone?'

'I will, directly I've got you home.'

He hunched himself as far away from the girl as possible. This would be a further shock for Antonia. Let her try and explain this away, let her find the reassuring answer, laugh it off. She would know the truth, that there was no harm in it. And yet was it perhaps more likely that she would think the girl was the important thing; the girl, and not him?

'Anyway,' the girl said vaguely, looking up from her shoes, 'I've got to be here this evening.'

'Here? Where?'

'Hampstead.'

'It's only lunch time.'

'No,' she said, looking at her watch, 'it's three o'clock.'

'Even so . . .' He was going to say that it was a long time, too long, till the evening, but after two words he asked himself bitterly why it mattered; why, inevitably, he should find himself worrying again about time, about where she was going and what she was going to do till then. He clenched his teeth, screwed up his aching eyes in the effort to feel again what he had felt while reaching for the dog. If only he could be alone. For God's sake, if only he could ever be alone, left alone. 'Get out!' he shouted suddenly. 'Go away! Get out!' He started rapping on the window. 'Stop! Stop here!'

Resigned, the taxi driver drew into the kerb. He didn't think he'd make it; surprised they'd got this far. He waited without turning round.

'Now,' Mark said, 'go away. I'm sorry, but you must go.' He opened the door for her. She hesitated, perched sideways on the seat.

'Have you got any money?'

He was patient. 'Yes.'

'All right.' She seemed to have made up her mind about something, not only to leave him. She got out and firmly closed the door, even trying the handle to see that it was properly shut. He could see the wooden latches of her duffle coat, and then she moved away from the window. Although for a moment he wanted to, he did not look back. The taxi driver, staring straight ahead, let in the clutch.

'All right?'

'Yes,' said Mark. His objective was Antonia and to present to her undimmed, immediately, his madness. He felt no regret for the girl, only relief that she had gone.

They entered the park. Men hurried their children across the road. The sun had gone; there would be no sunset, no dusk, only the sudden appearance of night. Possibly Antonia would think him ill enough to go to bed. He sheered resolutely away from the picture of himself sleeping, a hot-water bottle, Georgina made to whisper and walk on her toes, the house being quietly put to rights about him. The effort must continue to bore down, drill deep, unearth the truth, but trying to think was like drilling into cloud; the thoughts slipped; the effort was immense and useless.

The fact was, he knew, that there was no decision to be made; there was no choice. He did not have to choose between being what he had been all his life and what this afternoon he had suddenly become. His life was absolutely without alternatives. He had never had to decide anything, only make the distinction between what was possible and what was not. He had not decided to love Antonia, have four children, be moderately successful, live and perhaps die in Sheldon Road. All these things had been within his scope, possible; not to do them would have been difficult, required thought. If he was in fact wondering whether he was the man who had stared at him out of the mirror, he was wasting his time. He did not have to decide against being a murderer.

The taxi turned into Sheldon Road. Mark put his handkerchief away, straightened his tie. So that was it, he thought calmly. Nothing very strange, really; a desire that must come to everyone at some time in their life, or so he had heard. Only madmen actually took the responsibility. He fussed with himself, uselessly trying to disguise his torn shirt, brush the blood and dust off his jacket. He no longer wanted to shock Antonia. He was already deeply moved by her sympathy and understanding. He did not want to hurt her unnecessarily. In the middle of a Sunday afternoon she was to deliver him from madness, and this would require all her skill. Considerately, he would not indulge in dramatics.

He paid the driver and waited until the taxi had disappeared round the corner. The street was empty, deserted already for the night. Fog, so far no more than a thickening and dampening of air, was coming; the dustbin lids, the black branches of the ash tree, the chipped front steps glistened, slimed by the trail of fog. The house, piled up square and shut against the heavy sky, was without lights, but this was not remarkable since the Paintons, like everyone else in Sheldon Road, lived at the back and only the nursery and the children's bedroom looked out on to the street. Opening the gate, Mark longed suddenly to be released from what was to come; to be asked no questions, to sit down with the children at tea, to build great viaducts of bricks and postpone from hour to hour fetching the coal; to slip unnoticed into his place and say nothing. At the same time, and it was part of the same feeling, he longed to be a child again and be drawn indoors to crumpets and cocoa and bed; to be Georgina, who all day must have been smugly enjoying Antonia's love. He climbed noisily up the steps, carefully avoiding the pram, and unnecessarily scraped his key in the lock. The door swung open on darkness.

Nothing had been done. This was the first thing that he realised, as shocking as a church littered with yesterday's hymn books, empty wine bottles, crumbs of wafer. Nothing, since he left the house, had been done. He fell over the vacuum cleaner, abandoned in the hall; looked fiercely and quickly from the dead fire to the dirty glasses, to the tumbled sofa; switched on the lights and, stamping down to the kitchen, found greasy plates floating in cold water; pounded upstairs again to discover in the dark bedroom the bed unmade, the paraphernalia of morning tea—dirty crockery and spilt milk and electrical equipment—scattered on the floor; in the bathroom his pyjamas, damp and disgusting as a discarded skin, still lay in a heap, and there was a black rim round the bath, his own grime unpardonably not removed. 'My God!' he said out loud; and then, realising that there was no one to hear him, stamped his foot and shouted, 'My God!', allowing full strength to his outrage. There must be some explanation, a note by the telephone. Charlotte. Nothing less than disaster. He leapt down the stairs, switched on the sitting-room lights, searched through the papers on his desk, scattering them on either side: nothing. His hands were shaking, and he had to dial the number twice.

'Charlotte Painton. Painton. PAINTON.'

'Which ward, please?'

'A. Ward A, for God's sake.'

'Just a moment . . . Ward A?'

'Charlotte Painton. How is she? Is she all right?'

'Charlotte had her operation this morning. She is progressing satisfactorily.'

'But is she all right?'

'She is sleeping.'

'*But is she all right?*'

'She is perfectly all right, Mr Painton. She is sleeping.'

'Has her mother been in?'

'No one is allowed to see her today.'

'Her mother hasn't been there?'

'No, Mr Painton. No one is allowed to see her today.'

He brought his hand down on the telephone rest before dropping the receiver. Nothing, nothing, nothing. He recognised the sensation in his lungs, his throat, his eyes; he was going to weep. But, he thought, there is no one to hear me. The tears, the choking left him. He collapsed, shoulders slumped, hands slack, head hanging as on a broken neck. Slowly and rather heavily he walked across the room and stood by the mantelpiece, facing, without noticing it, the Matisse print. His eyes wandered across it, down to the mantelpiece: a dirty glass, a snapshot of Felicity, a small Dresden plate. He reached for the plate, turned it over, looked at the rivets where it had once been mended, stitches in a porcelain skin. He dropped it into the grate. The plate immediately smashed. He sat down in the wing chair and looked at the pieces.

For a long time, perhaps an hour, he did not move. The pattern of the broken pieces in the grate became printed on his mind, so that he could have arranged them again in exactly the same place or, if necessary, drawn a diagram showing each splinter and fragment of china in relation to the brass fender and fireplace. Outside, the fog gathered, the gardens sank, the light from the sitting-room windows shone on the iron struts of the swing, the sagging clothes-line. When at last Mark raised his head he saw that it was now night.

For the whole of his life expectation and satisfaction had been moderate; he had never hoped for more than he could receive; never, he thought, received more than he asked for. Today, for the first time, he had expected everything and had been given nothing; worse than nothing, for the empty, uncared-for house was to him a positive deprivation, a tearing from him of something he owned, part of his life. His suspected madness, his violence, had become during the drive home a gift which he was to present to Antonia. What was he to do with it now? What was he to do with himself? He moved his hands impotently, as though weighing the burden of nothing; stood up; walked a few steps across the room and stopped. A bell rang, a short scream in the silent house. He waited, his heart beating heavily, standing as still as a child in a wood. It rang again, and he moved cautiously towards the door. He was no longer prepared. He did not know what would happen, whether he would astonish, horrify or hurt her. He did not know what he would do, beyond opening the door. He only knew for certain that Antonia was there and that suddenly he was frightened.

He flung open the door quickly. The girl looked up, as though even in the fog, on the doorstep, she had been absorbed in her distant feet. 'Hullo,' she said; then, stepping towards him, 'Remember me?'

CHAPTER 17

DAVID'S sister was a strong, tall woman with large teeth and hair plaited on top of her head. She was full of oaths, laughed loudly, sat whenever possible on the floor, as cosy and coquettish as a giraffe. She was younger than Antonia and made her feel that she belonged not only to a different generation but a different species. For nearly two hours, drinking sherry, cheap red wine and now brandy, Antonia had hardly spoken except shyly, in a way confidentially to Annette. She sat in a canvas-and-iron chair deliberately designed for sitting in, a bar cutting her savagely behind the knees, her arms pinned to her sides, a deliberately designed space behind her head so that she could not lean back and felt the muscles of her neck turning to iron. Sometimes, with difficulty, she stubbed out a cigarette in an ashtray shaped like a beseeching hand; watched, through the bamboo fences and lively ivies, the outside world growing darker and more dense until the lights, unpretentious contortions of rubber and iron, were switched on and she was gently illuminated, golden as a Corregio and as unlikely.

The sister, Veronica, had a baby with straight orange

hair and a drooping mouth, in and out of which food poured, causing no change of expression, no shifting of the pale, pink-rimmed eyes. There was a Nanny, out, and a husband away: a cheerful-looking man from his photograph, something to do with television and not mentioned or enquired after by David. The gramophone had played ceaselessly since they arrived; played, as far as Antonia could tell, the same solemn, sexy lament over and over, although occasionally Veronica turned it louder, saying, 'You simply must listen to this,' and sometimes softer, explaining perfunctorily, 'Bill's.' Annette had piled cushions on the composition floor and was reading three comics she had thoughtfully brought with her. David lay, apparently comfortable, in a kind of deck-chair, his feet and legs reaching into the firelight, the upper part of his body in shadow; from time to time his hand would come down into the light and drop a cigarette-end in his coffee saucer, where it unfurled like a Japanese flower. Having introduced Antonia with no explanation as to why he had brought her, he seemed to have cut her loose, let her sink or swim in the tide of Veronica's incessant talk. She had, she realised with shame, sunk like a stone. She had begun in the last half hour to feel angry with him, as though it were he who had dragged her here against her will. She would have been angry with more reason if she had known of the telephone conversation that had been going on while she hurried out of the park.

'I'm bringing a girl along.'

'Oh.' She had wanted him to herself, luxuriously

planning to talk the whole afternoon about her marriage. 'Barbara?'

'No. Mrs Mark Painton. Mother of four.'

'You must be mad. A girl, I thought you said.'

'Be nice to her. Lay on the drink.'

'You'll pay.'

'I'll pay, but behave yourself.'

'Why the hell should I? Find lunch somewhere else.'

'We'll be round in half an hour.'

'And her name is?'

'Antonia.'

'Toni, something like that?'

'Simply Antonia.'

And for the first half an hour, unknown to Antonia, she had tried to behave herself, both impressed and intimidated by the tall, slim, slow woman in the rather countrified tweed suit, by the gentle, nervous face which at first kept turning towards David and later looked only at Annette and the baby; impressed also by David, whose taste, she thought, had changed in some way alarmingly for the better. She wondered, briefly and without real interest, what he hoped to get out of it. After half an hour she had come to the conclusion that whatever he hoped for he would get nothing, was wasting his time. She felt vaguely sorry for Antonia for being so out of touch, so obviously unsatisfactory, but a great deal more irritated by her aloofness—her, as Veronica would put it with school-girl scorn, sniffiness. As she herself had not been shy since she was a small child, as she had so far bounded through life with the verve and savagery of an inept

163

hockey player, she considered all quiet women sniffy, bristled at the suspicion that inwardly they were criticising her, although if they were it was of course from envy. Her kind heart was constantly baffled by ignorance, inability to recognise fear or tenderness or contentment. A dark winter afternoon, cold dregs of coffee, hot fire, gramophone, was to her the core, the innermost sanctuary of life. Entering a room containing all these things, she felt like an initiate come home after a short, dismal excursion into the daylight world to which she believed Antonia belonged.

David looked at both women from the neutrality of his patch of darkness; he realised that they disliked each other and vaguely, without bothering to think about it, understood why. Crossing the threshold of the Paintons' house two days ago, he had been cautious and curious as a man wondering whether to settle in new territory. As a woman, Antonia did not particularly interest him. She was the embodiment of all the mysteries which in his own marriage had remained unsolved, a native of a world he had briefly seen and at the time disliked, frightened then by the peculiar dangers, rigid laws, the terrifying possibility of instant destruction which now in middle age he found fascinating. Antonia had lived, as he might have done, in a state of sensuality and hate, as well as in the common air of love. She was well up in the hierarchy of a society in which everything was permissible except chastity; this, at the moment, intrigued him. He had kissed her yesterday out of simple curiosity; at dinner he had been disappointed because she had obstinately avoided talking about Mark and the children, but his interest had soon revived once they got back to find the house empty, children gone, Mark making a fool of himself. He had wondered, much as he might have wondered reading the script of a film in which later he might be involved, how it was all going to turn out. His sister, being a woman and only interested in getting him married and suffering as she did, naturally did not understand.

'Antonia.'

'Yes?' She looked up quickly, like someone who has been waiting for a command.

'You're very quiet.'

'I'm sorry.' She turned to Veronica with her most nervous, most visitor-like smile, ready to carry her disappointment away with her untouched. 'I must go. It was so nice of you—'

'Nonsense.' David got up like a man getting out of bed, stretching, shaking himself into activity. 'Why do you have to go?'

'It's late.'

'Late. Late. Late for what?'

'Time to do Susan,' Veronica sighed, as though doing Susan was some obscure and difficult operation like doing the accounts. 'I've only just done her, I'm sure.' She got up reluctantly, her body snapping into a standing position in sections. She groaned, feeling her joints. 'I can't understand why Nanny has to go out. She comes back perfectly miserable.'

'I'll say goodbye, then,' Antonia said. There was

hardly room for all three of them standing on the hearthrug; they were awkwardly close together, as though on a raft. Annette, from her island on the far side of the room, looked up hopefully. 'Are we going, then?'

'No, no.' Veronica was desperate at the idea that they should follow Antonia, leaving her alone. 'Please don't go. Susan won't take a minute. Darling, come and help me bath Susan.' She held out her hand to Annette, grateful even for the child's company during the long banishment to the bathroom and nursery. Annette got up eagerly. Retarded in every way by her father, her Lilliputian world inhabited by imaginary children to whom she talked, unnaturally lisping, in the dark and lonely evenings when she was put too early to bed, she adored her cousin Susan; envied her for being a genuine baby, was excited by the para-phernalia of talcum powder and soiled nappies, belch-ing and small knitted boots. But she bargained, a natural enemy of her aunt, 'May I hold her?'

'Yes. Yes, I suppose so.' Veronica lit a cigarette; it would burn itself out in an ashtray propped on the side of the bath. 'But, David, don't go. Toni, stay and keep him company. Have a drink. Play the gramophone. Please stay.' She offered her greatest treasures in despair that they might leave her, forget-ting that the drink was finished, the records already repeating themselves for the third time. 'I'm sure you have Nannies and things to cope with the children.'

'She hasn't any children,' David said. 'They've all left.'

166

'Then,' Veronica said, concerned only with her own problem and not at all with the vision of four children leaving Antonia suddenly, without reason, 'then that's all right. She can stay.'

'Will you?' David asked.

She turned to him, her breath caught in exasperation. She felt trapped by the three of them, all fastening on her for their own purposes, disregarding the obvious fact that she wanted to go, to return, if not to Mark then to her abandoned house, to find in it some satisfaction, some justification for the dying day. 'But—' she began. David reached out his hand and closed it over hers; she looked down in surprise, feeling the hard clutch of his hand, detaining and at the same time demanding. She tried to pull her hand away, smiling at Annette, whose criticism she feared more than the rest. 'Shall I, Annette?' It was a cowardly way out, and the child, knowing it, simply nodded, deciding, with this indifferent movement of her head, much of her own future.

CHAPTER 18

W HEN they had gone David kept her hand for a moment, as though she might decide to follow them. Then he abandoned her, walking quickly to the other side of the room and inspecting the empty bottles on the table.

'The drink's all gone,' he said. 'Bill's the meanest man I know, never keeps any drink in the house; all there is I bring.'

'It doesn't matter.' She sat down with relief on the more comfortable sofa. 'We've been drinking ever since lunch.'

'Do you want the gramophone on?'

'I don't mind.'

'We've heard all these before.' He looked at both sides of two records, reading the titles. 'I like opera. Do you?'

'No,' Antonia said, smiling.

'Pity. I like opera.' He picked up two more records, holding them like cymbals he was about to beat together. 'I didn't want you to go. I'm having a party this evening. Why don't you come?'

'No, I— Really, I must go home.'

'Why? Mark's gone, you said.'

'But I must go home all the same.'

He switched the gramophone on, asking, with his back to her, 'Why did you quarrel?'

'I don't think we did, exactly.'

He came over and stood in front of the fire, his hands in his pockets, looking down at her. 'My wife and I quarrelled often. I think out of boredom. I used to wonder whether in time we would—you know—wear each other out. Sometimes I hated her. Is that usual?'

'When did you hate her?'

'Oh, at the times when, if I hadn't been married to her, I wouldn't have seen her. When she cut her toenails, stopped locking the bathroom door. She had one hair used to grow out of a mole on her neck. For some time I didn't notice it, then she started pulling it out when I was there, in the bedroom. She was beautiful, small and thin like Annette. It didn't make any difference. You know?'

'Do you miss her very much?' Antonia asked uneasily.

'Not now. And yet if I did miss her it would be because of those things, I think. Not because I loved her or anything like that. Not at all.' He came and sat down beside her on the sofa, taking her hand and turning the wedding ring round and round on her finger. 'You think all marriages are like that?'

'I don't know.'

'You think I should try it again?'

'Do you want to?'

'Yes. Yes, I think I do.' He turned easily, comfortably, like a man turning in bed, and lay with his head on her thighs, his feet propped on the arm of the sofa. She sat as still as though a small bird had suddenly hopped on to her lap. He said, 'Mark must have a very pleasant life.'

'Why?'

'What goes on between you two? Why have you got all those children? Is he faithful to you?'

'Why do you want to know?'

'I don't know. In case I ever try it myself, I suppose.' With one finger he traced the outline of her breast, his fingernail making a small scraping on the silk of her blouse. 'I suppose it would be good for Annette.'

'If you married.'

'Yes. Or you could adopt her. Adopt both of us.'

She felt as though she was balancing on a tightrope; the slightest movement and she would be lost—even this, outrageous and painful though it was, would be lost. Her whole body hurt with the effort of keeping still. She pressed her head against the back of the sofa, looking away from him. 'Who would you marry?'

'Oh, there's a girl. You wouldn't like her.'

'Why not?'

He pushed himself upright and sat with his arm loosely round her shoulders, so that it was impossible for her to remain rigid—she had to slacken and settle within the curve of his arm. The movement, as she had felt it would, dislodged her. Reluctantly, with the same sensation as though she were falling, she raised her face. He looked back at her, smiling a little, making no effort to help her but curious as to what she would do next. Then with a slight shrug of his shoulders he tightened his arm and kissed her, drawing back immediately to look at her face, as though he had sketched on it the shape of his mouth. 'You wouldn't,' he said. 'That's all.'

Words tumbled out purposelessly; she didn't care about the girl. 'But why do you think so? She's probably'—she picked a word at random, throwing it at him—'charming.'

He laughed. 'I don't like her much myself. She's vicious and untidy and far too young.'

'Then why—?'

'Just one of those things.' One hand on her thigh, the other on the back of her neck beneath the loose, heavy coil of hair, he pulled her gently towards him. With a sudden petulance, following the unalterable curve of her fall, she wrenched away and got up.

'It's absurd. I should never have phoned you. It's'—she threw out her hand desperately—'absurd.'

'Why?'

'Of course it is! What do you want with someone like me?'

'What's the matter with you?'

'Nothing.'

'Then come and sit down again. Don't be silly.'

'But—'

'Look,' he said. 'I'm not going to fight to get you.' He smiled gently, as though imparting some unfortunately true information. 'Why don't you come and sit down?'

She was beginning to cry. The grief in her, which could only appear as small, ugly tears, was at that moment the despair of all women for something gone, never to come again—something never known, now never to be known. She wrapped her arms round herself and stood with her head bent, hiding her face from him, fighting with herself for pride, for the gift of lying. After a few moments she walked over to the gramophone and switched it off, waiting until the record expired into silence. She said, 'She doesn't sound as though she'd be much good with Annette.'

His voice was relieved. 'Oh, I think she'll do. I spoil her, you know.'

'Annette?'

'Yes. Guilt or something. Tell me about Mark.'

'Mark?'

'What does a man like that feel? You know, I look at him and I wonder how he ever brought himself to have all those children. He's madly in love with you, I suppose?'

'Be quiet!' She turned so quickly that he flinched, as though she had thrown something at him across the room. Her whole body seemed to have become smaller, lighter; her hair had fallen round her face, making it look thin, young, almost vicious in anger.

'I'm sorry.' He got up, unwinding his legs slowly, keeping his eyes on her. 'I'm sorry, I didn't know you felt like that. Is that how you feel?'

'What right have you got to— Oh, you don't know what you're talking about, you don't know anything. What right have you got to talk about Mark like that? How dare you!'

For the first time he concentrated on her, careful and intent. He approached her cautiously, picking his way among the lamps and tables, through the sparse forest of ivy. She watched him coming with enormous, startled eyes, her lips parted, her body ready to spring away. He reached out and caught her hand, coaxing her towards him. 'Is that it? Is that what's wrong?'

She didn't care any more. As in a dream in which you love the improbable, the impossible, person, in which there is no barrier to desire, she stretched her arms and closed them round him, meeting him so closely that at last he was alive, urgent, demanding, impatient for her, as though he too had been waiting for many years.

When he looked up he saw Annette, her mouth half open, transfixed, staring at him from the doorway.

173

H E pushed Antonia away so violently that she stumbled and fell against the sofa.

'What are you doing?' he shouted. 'What the hell are you doing?'

The child could not answer; she was doing nothing. She simply stood and looked, her eyes moving to Antonia and back again to her father. She had not understood what she had seen; it was his anger that made her think something terrible had happened and that this was in some way concerned with her and that she was somehow, for the first time in her life, in a position of power. She did not know what to do and thought it safest to stay where she was and keep looking, since this had such effect.

'You come barging in!' David blustered. 'Why the hell do you come barging in? What do you want? Why don't you stay in the nursery? Where's Veronica?'

'Don't—' Antonia began. Remorselessly the child's eyes moved towards her, raked up and down from the tangled hair, over the crumpled, gaping clothes to the stockinged feet. Having silenced the interruption, Annette turned again to David.

'I'm sorry,' she said. 'I thought it might be time

to go.' She moved just enough to show a pink toy rabbit she was holding. 'Veronica said I could have this.'

The rabbit was far more important to her than the peculiar but uninteresting idea that her father, when left alone with women, kissed them. The rabbit was an acquisition. She was looking forward to taking it home and feeding it on small quantities of corn-flakes from a plastic saucer. She had already decided with some excitement to call it Cuddlepie. Rightly believing that her father liked these sweet names she found for her toys, she though that she might placate him.

'I thought,' she said, lisping carefully, 'I would call him Cuddlepie.'

She looked down fondly at the rabbit. The most terrible thing in her life happened when it was suddenly snatched out of her hand and thrown violently across the room. One moment it was there, round and pink and coy in her hand; the next moment it was hurtling through the air; the next moment both she and Antonia had plunged towards it where it lay, stomach upwards, in the tangle of flex behind the gramophone.

She thought, not unnaturally, that Antonia was supporting her father and trying to take the rabbit from her. She kicked energetically with her square laced shoe, reached for the rabbit with one hand and with the other grabbed at the ropes of flex. The gramophone and the fragile table, with its insect legs, crashed together. Annette stamped about among the scattered records, screaming. Antonia, drawing in her breath and throwing herself backwards as though from the edge of a precipice, began uncontrollably to laugh. David's voice was raised higher, like a preacher desperately continuing a sermon to a congregation in revolt. 'How old are you?' he kept demanding. 'Ten? How old are you? Ten?' The noise brought Veronica eagerly from the nursery, the baby limp on her hip. She saw her records being trampled; Antonia, with undone hair, laughing, bent as though in pain over the back of the sofa; David turning this way and that, flaying his arms like a gigantic scarecrow and bawling his senseless question into each corner of the room. She uttered a short sound, a bark of outrage, and collared Annette, who continued to kick with convulsive, ecstatic rage, her face screwed tight and red round the gaping square of her mouth. Antonia, shaken with the last weary sob of laughter, looked directly into the baby's cold, unwavering eyes. When she straightened herself, without attempting to smooth her hair or arrange her clothes, she had strangely resumed the appearance known to her own children, as though a strong current, temporarily blocked, was flowing again.

She walked past Veronica and the child, who seemed now to be fighting for some forgotten cause, picked up the rabbit out of the debris and handed it to David. Then, taking her shoes, jacket and handbag, she went out of the room.

The rest of the flat had been left to chance. The bedroom which Antonia found was large, bare, and squalid. An enormous mirror, clouded with dust and the damp air, was propped in a corner; the divan bed was unmade, one of its legs supported by an encyclopaedia of sexual knowledge; the two chairs were heaped with the week's clothes, and the dressing-table was covered with a fine dust of powder and cigarette ash. Through the open, curtainless window the fog poured as though from a dark tunnel, settling on the grey sheets and hairy rugs on the bed, on the bare electric-light bulb, mildewing the depressing library of love supported between two ebony elephants on the marble mantelpiece.

Antonia shivered. Her body ached, she could hardly raise her arms to comb and plait and twist the burden of her hair. Trained for bearing children, nursing children, crouching and stretching, climbing and bending, running, moving in a thousand small, complicated gestures, she was now stiff, cramped, aching. Carefully and slowly she did her hair, went out to the bathroom and washed her face with a sliver of gritty soap such as is found in train lavatories, came back and arranged her powder compact, lipstick, and mascara on the corner of the mantelpiece, like a surgeon placing instruments ready for an operation. Before facing herself in the mirror she buttoned her blouse, pulled it down tight under her skirt, carefully rolled up the crumpled sleeves, put on her shoes. Then, swiftly, she wheeled round to the mirror as though to catch herself unawares.

She made her face up as carefully as she had done everything else. There was no hesitation in her movements; they were slow with fatigue, but certain. When she had finished she packed her handbag again, snapped it shut, folded her jacket over her arm and left the room, her back dwindling into a white speck in the long, misty corridor of the mirror.

The telephone was in the hall. She could hear voices still raised in the sitting-room, punctuated by small, indefinite screams. She lifted the receiver and dialled the number, already drawing in her breath to speak. While the ringing tone went on and on, seeming sometimes to falter and then continue even more insistently, she remembered without remorse the state in which she had left the house that morning. The house no longer meant anything to her: it was a myth in which, disillusioned but without rancour, she no longer believed. She thought of it only as a receptacle for the shrilling telephone, a small, black, palpitating heart alive in the dead and dusty wreckage of walls and landings. It was with a kind of awe that she at last realised it would not be answered. She was not surprised; only for a moment at a loss, like someone stopping to feel their way in the dark.

She was replacing the receiver as the sitting-room door opened and the voices became abruptly louder, quarrelling, furious, the voices of two people who have long ago taken off from reason and now toss about, unearthed, directionless. David was carrying Annette. Her legs still jerked convulsively, she was stiff in his arms, her head turned away from him. Behind him, Veronica's head appeared as though stretched out on a neck like a coiled spring. Her

178

vituperation seemed to Antonia as meaningless and absurd as the cursing of a medieval witch; based on the destruction of her gramophone records, it extended back to childhood and forward to an obscene vision of David's old age. The verve and accuracy of her hate was that of a little girl for an elder brother; the absurdity was in the fact that she was too old for it, too large, too awkward and too old. David came forward, holding the child as though forced by a pistol in his back. Seeing Antonia, he stopped, then hurried on again as his sister burst out of the room behind him. He held the child out as though he would topple her from his arms into Antonia's.

'She's awfully upset,' he said. 'I can't do anything with her.'

'You never can!' Veronica screamed. 'I can't do anything with her! Nanny can't do anything with her! I tell you—'

'Oh, shut up,' David said wearily. He spoke hesitantly to Antonia, as though she were a stranger he had fortunately come upon. 'I thought you'd gone. I suppose you wouldn't be so kind—with these people coming in—difficult like this—I don't think I can cope.'

'Yes,' Antonia said. Although he was the stronger, it seemed natural to them both that she should carry the child. She held out her arms and locked them firmly round the stiff, small body. David followed without looking back, holding the pink rabbit like a useless trophy he had won in some dissolute, adult carnival.

CHAPTER 20

THE girl solemnly dressed herself, even to the armoured duffle coat. While she was dressing she kept her back turned to him, a thin back still shadowed with last summer's sunburn. The short, solid legs raised and bent as she stepped into her clothes with concentrated, heavy movements, like someone climbing a steep slope. She dressed the lower part of her body first, bent and fastened her shoes, then stood carefully upright, as though balancing, and fastened the white strip of her brassiere, fastening it back to front and swivelling it round so that for a moment it hung empty on her back like the shreds of wings. Then she raised her arms and plunged into her enormous sweater. She did not turn round until, safely at the summit, she had latched her coat.

'Is there anything I can do?'

'Do?' Mark flung his legs off the sofa, pushed himself upright. He looked at the open palms of his hands. 'You mean anything more you can do?'

'I'm sorry.'

'I'm sorry. I didn't mean it like that. You sounded like—' He looked up at her uncertainly. 'What sort of thing?'

She laughed shortly, almost soundlessly. 'I don't know what you mean. Really I don't. I have to go soon, and I wondered if there was anything I could do for you. Like making tea.'

'Tea?'

'Why not? They say it steadies the nerves.'

He shrugged his shoulders, looking at her in bewilderment. 'All right. If you like, make tea.'

He watched her go out of the room and then sat motionless, like someone who has been left, unwillingly helpless, while a companion searches for food. He heard her going down the basement stairs and then there was silence, he was alone again.

She had said 'Remember me?' and stepped into the hall as though she had come with a purpose, as though he had been expecting her. Why he had held her he could not now remember: to prevent her coming in; to support himself, because for a moment he had felt like falling; to welcome her, drag her eagerly in; to injure her, as he had the dog? He could only remember that as he had grasped her arms and looked down at her inquisitive, stupid little face he had felt a tremendous surge of comfort, relief such as an exhausted swimmer might feel when the final wave, more powerful, more certainly destructive than all the rest, begins to break and the agonising exercise of hope becomes no longer necessary.

She, on the other hand, had seemed quite certain. She had not flinched or pulled away, but while he was still undecided had put her arms round his neck and guided his head until his mouth was on hers. If she had shown the slightest doubt he could have as easily hurt her: the desire to destroy and the desire to possess were, in that second of anticipation, equal and separate. What, if she had been Antonia, would have been dissipated in love, reproach, confession, the familiar and shallow harbour, became dangerous and extreme. For a moment he grasped her shoulders too tightly; then desire left his hands and burst through his entire body, and just as the girl was not Antonia he was no longer himself but separate and lonely, as at the moment of birth or death.

He sat motionless, waiting not only for the girl to come back but for his own strength to return. He was empty, scoured, clean. Wisps of thought drifted through him, soft and easy as air drifting through the bleached arches of a human skull. The ringing of the telephone sounded, for a time, very distant. When he got up and went over to his desk it was more like a memory than something he was actually doing.

'Mr Painton?'

'Yes.'

'This is Mrs Greenbaum, Daniel's mother. I thought you might be wanting to hear from Georgina.'

'It's very kind of you.' He heard and recognised the mounting scream of the kettle. 'How is she?'

'She's very much better. After Mrs Painton left this morning she slept for a while and woke up right as rain. I gave her a nice tea and then she and Daniel watched television. I'm just going to make her a nice cup of Horlicks and pop her into bed. I thought you might be worrying.'

'It's so kind of you,' Mark repeated. He pushed his fingers up over his forehead, through his thin hair, in a gesture distantly remembered; his precise, cultured voice was heard, recognised as on a forgotten gramophone record. 'Mrs Painton was there when? This morning?'

'Well, yes, she left about half-past twelve. I hope she didn't mind Georgina staying, but I always think children know what's best for them, and after the shock—'

'Of course,' Mark said. 'I didn't know. I've been— working. And Mrs Painton is at the hospital. So I didn't really know.' Quickly, before she could speak again, he asked, 'Is Georgina there?'

'She's in the lounge watching television,' Mrs Greenbaum said testily, suspiciously, as though she had told him countless times.

'Could I speak to her?'

To this there was no reply except a distant shriek, a parrot call, 'Georgina! Georgina!' He heard the girl coming upstairs with the tray, the slight rattle of china as she found her way in the dark. As she came into the room, holding the tray carefully at chest level, Georgina said 'Hullo,' her breathing so close that it seemed to warm, to irritate his ear. 'Daddy? Is that you?'

'Yes. Hullo.' He turned his back on the girl. 'How are you? Are you better?'

'I'm all right.'

'Mummy came to see you?'

'Yes.'

'Good. Charlotte's all right.'

'Oh.'

'Are you having a nice time?'

'Yes, thank you.'

'Are you going to bed now?'

'Yes, I think so.'

'Coming home tomorrow?'

'Yes.'

'Well. Everything's all right here.'

'Is Mummy there?'

'No. She's gone down to see Charlotte. Well, I just wanted to know you were all right.'

'Is Thomas back?'

'No, I don't think Thomas is back. I haven't seen him.'

'Oh. Goodbye, then.'

'Goodbye, Georgina.'

He turned round and saw the girl bending to pour tea. 'It was my daughter,' he said. 'Georgina. The one who ran away.'

'What for?' She had brought two cups, but no saucers; only one teaspoon.

'I told you this morning.'

'No, you didn't tell me. Sugar?'

'She's the eldest child,' he said.

'Yes?' Holding her cup in both hands, she sat down on the arm of the sofa and looked at her feet, turning them this way and that. 'Everyone seems to run away from you.'

'No,' he insisted. 'Not from me.'

'From you,' she said obstinately.

'No, no. I am only part of it.'

'Of what?'

He was silent for a moment. So much, now, was realised. He could see his life calm, stretching behind him; he knew the depths and dragging tides, the ceaseless pull of the surface which had at last discharged him, or out of which he had struggled in order to be what he now was, alone. He could understand, but he could not explain. To the girl, who had never known his life, it would all be meaningless. He said, 'I can't explain. All this.' He held out his hands, as though supporting on their flat palms the high toppling weight of the house above them. 'But much more than that. Much more.'

'It sounds terribly complicated. Why don't you drink your tea?'

'I don't much like tea.' He noticed suddenly that she was eating, stuffing a great slab of bread and marmalade into her mouth. It was the first time he had ever seen her eating, and he felt the same surprise, almost embarrassment, that he had felt when she looked at the corset advertisements. He asked curiously, 'Are you hungry?'

She nodded vigorously. She seemed in the last few minutes to have assumed something of the life of the house, to have taken on the habits of hunger and thirst, to feel, as he had always done, the need for perpetual nourishment. When she had licked her fingers she took an apple out of her pocket and bit into it neatly, with a noise like breaking wood. 'What are you going to do now?' she asked.

'I could walk out of this house with you and never come back. It would be possible.'

'Don't be silly. What about all your children? You don't seem to think of them much.' She was turning the apple round as she ate, nibbling it down to the core.

'I don't have to think of them. Any more than I have to think about my arms or my legs.'

'Well, you wouldn't get very far without your arms or your legs.' She gave him a quick, triumphant look, settling it.

'But I could still live.'

'They couldn't.' She threw the core into the fireplace and quite suddenly put her hand on the back of his head, not so much in affection as reassurance. 'Anyway, you wouldn't want to do that. You don't love me. I don't love you, for that matter.'

'Of course not. But love, you know, can . . .' Again, lacking words, his hands came slowly, powerfully together, crushing the air until they were locked and rigid. 'With you there was none of that.'

She stood up, her arms held out a little, stiffly, as though attempting a greater gesture. 'I'm sorry,' she said. 'I didn't think. I just thought you were unhappy and shouldn't be left alone. I don't expect you believe me.'

'Anyway,' his hands dropped and he smiled, 'there it is. In a way I'm very grateful to you.'

'But you expected Antonia. If it had been Antonia, would the same thing have happened?'

He shook his head.

'Why?'

For a moment many reasons flooded his mind; he was articulate, he could give many reasons, elaborate and rationalise, defend, justify and so keep avoiding the truth. He got up as though physically to get away. He crossed to the fireplace and, kneeling down, began to pick the pieces of china one by one out of the grate. When he had finished he raised himself and carried the pieces in his cupped hand across the room and dropped them in the wastepaper basket. Then he said, 'Because with Antonia it is no good.'

Again the quick, light 'Why?' which he could not answer. Nevertheless he knew, could answer truthfully to himself. Because she isn't like you. You come here alone and in the end you will go away. Everything there is of you can be seen, felt and possessed. But Antonia is everything. She is my life, my house and my children, my work, my time, my future. Can you hold all that in your arms? Can you, without feeling too keenly the triviality of what you want, which is simply to do this one act in private, to be alone with her for this one not very magnificent act? He moved his hand over the desk without touching it; slowly, as though he were divining the substance, in some way the presence, of Antonia. No man, he thought, could do it unless he was master of all this as well. His hand hovered, benedictory, uncertain, over the photographs, the inkstand, the telephone, the calendar, the gulls' feathers gathered for his pipe by the children on a grey beach in a wet August.

At last, knowing he would not answer, she asked, 'And now, what are you going to do?'

'About that?'

'Well, no. About everything.'

'Until Antonia comes back, I am not sure. It depends very much what has happened to her, doesn't it?'

'Why should anything have happened? She simply didn't want to stay in this dreadful house. I don't blame her.' Although she had been fully ready for some time, by tugging at her coat and settling deeper into her collar she gave the impression of again getting dressed. 'I don't think you should stay here either.'

She was at arm's length, and he could have touched her, but there was no need. He was beginning already to think of her as someone independent of him, someone who in a short time would even forget his name.

'Where are you going?'

'To meet some people.' She said this as though it was obvious, as though asking him where else she could possibly be going.

'People you like?'

'Not people. One only.'

'You mean there will only be one other person there?'

'Oh no. There will be a lot.'

'But if I came with you—'

'You can come if you like.'

He walked to the door, looking down the misty hall, up into the dark well of the staircase. Abandoned for one day, the house had become a ruin, as though all that held it together was ceaseless movement and sound, perpetual use. The top landings might be gaping to the night, nothing left there but a wilderness of iron and plaster drowned in fog. He thought of all it contained, as the owner of a sinking ship might think, with the calmness of extreme shock, of a heavy and worthless cargo. He realised all the things he had worked throughout his life to possess: toothmugs, coat hangers, pie dishes, dolls, chamber pots, crayons, cornflakes, bottles and boxes and tins and jars and baskets, tons of paper and tin and plastic, wood and wool. Behind him, the girl waited, not as she had done before, with impatience, knowing the outcome, but quietly, giving him time to make up his mind. He said, 'Supposing she comes back?'

'Leave her a note. She can ring you up if she wants to.'

'Will you write down the telephone number?'

'Yes. I will leave it here, by the telephone.'

She handed him a pencil. He looked at the piece of paper on which she had written the number. Without recognising it he began to write below the number in his neat, positive handwriting. He wrote, 'Dearest Antonia. I do not know yet whether what I have done matters. I do not know—' He stopped, holding the pencil. He tore what he had written off the paper and threw it away. At last he left only the number, un-explained. The girl had already opened the front door and was waiting on the steps, facing outwards towards the thick fog. It was an attitude, a shape now so familiar that he could not, would never be able to, remember her naked; only the shape, stubby, taut, imperative, waiting while he walked steadily down the hall towards her, walking like a man finally leaving and going down into the night, thinking, 'I do not know yet whether what I have done matters.'

Some minutes after they had gone the telephone began to ring. It rang for a little while, and when it stopped the sound continued: the thin, plaintive mewing of a cat as it pushed and rubbed uselessly against the dark walls.

CHAPTER 21

As Mrs Levington read aloud, imbuing with tragedy and passion the rather sordid tale of a homeless frog, her mind was occupied with the problem of death. Pregnant with death, she had the same anxieties: if it should happen now, it would be unfortunate; how would they all manage; what would I do at the first, the unmistakable signs? Her rashness at having the children to stay at this stage when she was, so to speak, at full term gave her a certain wicked pleasure. It was a dangerous flirtation with something she had hitherto regarded as an old friend; a risk which took the dullness out of dying. Nevertheless, she was not sure that she hadn't over-reached herself, gone too far. Her arm tightened round Edward's resisting body. Felicity, sprawled heavily on her lap, turned over the page. 'Go on.'

' "Croak," said the frog, "I am green and ugly, and I have no home to call my own. Will you give me a bed for the night, Mr Rabbit?" But Mr Rabbit said, "I have forty-five children; and, besides, I live in a deep dark hole in the earth . . ." ' Mrs Levington put down the book for a moment. 'What a lot of children,' she said vaguely, with slight outrage.

'Rabbits have a lot,' Felicity said. 'Go on.'

Wondering now about the weeks, the years after her death, trying to see Antonia old, to telescope time and include Antonia's age and dying in her own, she read on as though the frog were her greatest concern. She longed to be able to put the book away, somehow to gain some information from the children about the future. For the whole day she had been in this state of timelessness, so that she was not sure whether these children were her own or whether they were children who would be born long after she had died—Antonia's grandchildren, Felicity's grandchildren, fainter and ever fainter shadows of Alfred and herself, flickering, at last disappearing for ever.

'Go on,' Felicity said. 'Why do you keep stopping?'

' "Croak," said the frog, "I am green and ugly, and I have no home to call my own. Will you give me a bed for the night, Mr Owl?" But Mr Owl said, "I am out all night; and, besides, I live in a—" '

'Tree,' Felicity sighed. She slid off Mrs Levington's lap and wandered across the room. 'Go on.'

Mrs Levington said, 'No. We have had enough for tonight. We'll finish it tomorrow.' She shut the book and closed her eyes. Her arm was still round Edward's shoulders; he was limp now, hypnotised by the sluggish, sporadically leaping flames of the dying fire; his weight leaning against her seemed almost that of a grown man. I know nothing, she thought peacefully, without regret. There is nothing I can tell them. That will be for Antonia to do. Antonia will manage. The thought came like unction, the final certain peace, after which there were no more problems, no more questions, nothing to do but give up. At last she was relinquishing life, felt it like some tangible thing slipping away from her towards others. It was to her a proper desertion. The child grew heavier; she was now so light, so relieved of life, that she felt no discomfort. It was only when he moved that she felt suddenly cold, drained of the strength which he was taking with him across the room.

'Bedtime,' she said, opening her eyes. 'Felicity.'

'Why do I have to go to bed with Edward? Why do I have to have a bath? Why can't I have my supper downstairs? Why can't we have some more reading? Why do I have to go to bed *now* . . . ?'

'Come along.' She got up slowly, with some care. 'You must say goodbye to Alfred.'

Their eyes regarded her steadily, shining and cold as cats' eyes in the dark. She corrected herself calmly. 'You must say goodnight to Grandfather. Hurry now.'

They walked very slowly, reluctant rather than mutinous, out of the room and up the short flight of stairs into the dark hall with its stone-flagged floor, cold as a dairy, dark as a tomb. She walked behind them, resting her shadow on their squat, strong shadows, waiting while Felicity opened the door and light, smoke, music poured out as though from a den of abandoned gaiety, some bar or cellar of rollicking vice. Mr Levington looked up vaguely from the book which he had not been reading, said, through the din of Sibelius, 'Ah,' seeing two children standing in the doorway and not remembering for the moment who they were.

'Good night,' Felicity said. She pulled at Edward, who, smelling the room of a man, edged forward ready to inspect, discover, possibly to be included. He shook off her hand and stepped into the ring of light. Mr Levington peered closer. He asked suddenly, 'Have you a train?'

'He has a train,' Felicity answered, 'but it is all broken up.'

'He could play with it in the attic.'

'But it is all broken up.'

'Yes,' Mr Levington said. He raised his book again, and Mrs Levington saw the children flow backwards towards her, saw the door close and felt them near her, undiminished, their energy pounding in the sudden enclosed darkness.

They raced, abruptly released, upstairs. They turned on all the lights; leapt on their beds and jumped and screamed and flew with outstretched arms and tore at their clothes and pushed her from one side to another, dodging her and thundering against her, knocking her like a shuttlecock from one end of the house to the other, from the great peeling bathroom with its roaring geyser to the bedroom, sending her scurrying, making her move with desperate, miraculous agility. 'Why?' they shouted. 'Why? Why? Why?' They stuck out their stomachs and strutted naked about the landing, pitiless like conquerors. They balanced, yelling for help, on the edge of the bath, ready to jump and destroy her.

'I am not strong, like your mother.'

'Why?'

'Because I am old.'

'So is she old.'

They leapt, landing one after the other like great cannon-balls in her lap. For a moment, seeing nothing but darkness and fighting in the darkness with their heavy bodies and hearing their breathing and shouting like that of a wild, invisible army, she thought that this was the end. The strength which at last flung them off and released her to sit upright, trembling and smiling and still holding the bath towel ready, was unsuspected and enormous. The children fell back and stood quiet while she dried them with careful, dabbing movements. Tentatively, Felicity began to question her again: Why do you grow old, die, love, weep, grow hungry, why do you live at all? 'You must ask your mother,' Mrs Levington said.

'Does she know?'

'Yes,' Mrs Levington said.

They both looked at her with the deep, almost religious respect felt by children at the moment when a ceremony reaches some extraordinary climax, a moment of unreality fixed for ever afterwards on the mind. Mrs Levington closed her eyes; her head dropped forward a little. The last drops of bath-water sighed away and there was silence—such silence that the light pouring out of the electric bulb seemed to hum, to be an audible brilliance.

'She's asleep,' Felicity whispered. 'We won't wake her.'

With great caution she opened the bathroom door, paused to take Edward's hand. When she had shut the door again she felt very unhappy.

'Why can't we go home?' she asked.

Edward looked at her mutely.

'I think,' she answered, 'we shall be going home tomorrow.'

CHAPTER 22

WHEN they arrived at his home David offered
to carry Annette. She clung to Antonia. So it
was a laboured, silent procession that climbed
up the stairs, Antonia lifting each foot slowly and
strongly, resting on the landings where numbered
doors were shut and hydrangeas were abundant in
brass coffins, feeling the deep carpet and warm air, as
though in a dream she was carrying a heavy child
through some strange, luxuriant landscape. At the last
stop she looked up and saw, through the trellis of
bleached banisters, eyes, shining and inquisitive, peering down at her; then heads, shoulders, hands fluttering
like white bats in the dark. Somebody laughed. David
pressed a light switch, and as she started to climb again
she saw sharp, smiling faces bent downwards and, on a
level with her face, the brilliant, trailing pennant of a
woman's stole. David passed her, brushing by and
running on, leaving her to come slowly, alone. She
heard him apologising, laughter, broken sentences, like
the sudden outbreak of birds, and then the sound drifting away through the opened door as she climbed
doggedly on and at last reached the top landing and
followed them, standing in the doorway watching

David as he hurried about turning on lights and fires, drawing curtains, apologising, knocking into his guests.

'Where shall I put her?' she asked.

'Oh God, I'm sorry.' He was helpless and distracted. 'You couldn't possibly put her to bed?'

A woman turned and asked eagerly, 'Why, what's the matter with Annette?' giving Antonia a quick, non-committal smile in case she turned out to be a governess or a foreign help. 'She looks very pale.'

Annette stared at her listlessly, becoming paler. David said, 'She's tired, just tired.' The guests, still in their overcoats, glanced towards them with some impatience: women flicked cold little smiles over their mouths and looked across them with hard eyes, thinking that David should organise things better; the men furtively searched for signs of drink; two script writers, who had not been getting on very well together, raised their eyebrows at each other and felt a sudden warmth. 'If you could,' David repeated urgently, 'put her to bed?'

Antonia looked at him steadily. In the last few hours she seemed to have come a long way, as though through a maze in which, though the distance is short, one can walk the circumference of the earth. She was very tired. She knew that there was still some way to go, although how far and in what direction she could not tell. She was astonished that having been travelling so long, so far, she should again find herself in this familiar place, in the doorway of a crowded room, with a child in her arms. The centre of the room, among the outwardly staring strangers, was the place she had been trying to reach: to get there seemed impossible. As though until now she had been blindfolded, she blinked her eyes a little, turned to the woman who was still, with faint distaste, peering down at Annette as though the child was some unidentified object at the bottom of a trench or well made by Antonia's arms. She looked back at David, who only a short time ago had made love to her. She looked down at the child, who regarded her dully, without appeal, taking her for granted, as though she had recognised in Antonia the texture, colour, odour of long discipline. 'No,' she said. 'I think you should put her to bed yourself.'

'What?'

'I think you should put her to bed yourself. Stand up, Annette.'

'But I asked you—I told you—'

'I know. I'm tired.'

'Well, really!' the woman said. Everyone was looking at Antonia. She felt them condemning her, outraged as though by some rebellious servant. None of the others spoke; none of them moved to help, to attempt the task themselves. The women were shocked, feeling awkward and betrayed; the men embarrassed, glancing sidelong at Antonia; only the two script writers were bored and bewildered, offering each other cigarettes and yawning round like spectators at some foreign sport.

'Very well,' David said. His mouth was tight, pursed in disgust. 'I suppose you want to go home.'

'No,' Antonia said. 'Not yet.'

'Then perhaps'—the sarcasm was heavy, ludicrous— 'you will look after my guests?'

'If you tell them where the drink is,' Antonia said, 'I'm sure they can look after themselves.' She smiled, fear beating heavily against her chest.

'Of course,' a man said loudly. There was a titter; they moved, changing their positions, looking away, relaxing the taut silence. Made bold, the same man added, 'You get on with your chores, old chap. Don't mind us,' and the woman moved petulantly, suddenly, away, snapping, 'Well, really!' as though it were a matter of principle.

For the second time that day Antonia struggled with fear and laughter. As an adult, she felt the whole thing to be absurd: she could take hold of Annette and propel her off to bed with no effort at all; the shocked hostility was ridiculous, could not possibly be real. On the other hand, she was frightened, setting herself not only against David and the uneasy room but against herself, against everything that she had ever been. Awkwardly, like a child who has gone too far, she turned and pretended to look with interest at the bookcase. Out of the corner of her eye she saw the open door, the way of escape; behind her she felt the group of strangers knotted tightly together, as though assembling themselves against her.

'Won't you have a drink?'

'No, thank you. No, I'm just going.'

'I've brought one for you.'

'Thank you, but really—'

He had, however, put it in her hand. She glanced at him timidly, seeing a benevolent middle-aged face, a massive body slightly, courteously, inclined towards her.

'You live near here?'

'Yes, quite near.'

'I haven't seen you before, have I?'

'No. No, I don't think so.'

'We had difficulty in getting up here from Chelsea. The fog is very thick.'

'Yes. Yes, it is.'

There was a silence. He seemed to be musing, gently drifting on the current of some comfortable thought. Suddenly he asked, 'Are you in films?'

'Oh no.' A moment's hesitation and then, with difficulty, 'Are you?'

'No.' He leant against the bookcase, looking sideways down at her while she stood still with her back to the room, her head bent. 'I think most people here are.'

'Yes, I expect so.'

'They move about, you know, from place to place. Like a herd. This morning I saw most of them on the other side of London. Now, of course, they've changed their clothes.'

She looked down at her blouse, skirt, flat shoes. This morning at Mrs Greenbaum's, on the bus, in the sunlight as long ago as summer, they had been part of her. Now they were outgrown, old-fashioned, belonging to another season. She said quickly, 'I didn't know I was coming to a party. In fact, I'm not. I mean, I haven't. I really must go.' She put down her empty glass. He said, 'But you look charming,' neatly taking another glass from a passing tray and putting it into her hand. 'Don't protest. I know you are capable of it.' His face increased its gentleness, tenderly beaming with a direct and innocent warmth. 'Tell me, have you known David long?'

'Not very long.'

'Your husband isn't here? No, of course not. I saw you come up the stairs. Tell me, why didn't you want to put the child to bed?'

'She was upset. She doesn't know me very well. I thought it would be better if David—'

'You felt you were being put upon. Your maternal instinct does not, with little Annette, function? Presumably maternal attraction, like sex attraction, is discriminating? You don't want to fall into bed with every child you meet?'

'No,' Antonia said, smiling at last. His coaxing successful, he too smiled with mild delight over the rim of his glass. 'You are perfectly right,' he said. 'The child is, in any case, a little monster. Tell me, then—what do you do?'

'I do nothing. I mean, I have no job.'

'Nothing? You mean you don't even make lampshades, write little stories for the women's magazines? You mean you do *nothing*?'

'Yes,' she said. 'That's right. I really do nothing.'

'But don't you get very bored?'

'No.'

'My wife,' he said, his voice tinged with quiet melancholy, 'runs a hat shop. She loathes it, of course. But you live entirely on your husband?'

'How do you know I am married?' she asked, suddenly raising her head, boldly.

'My dear girl—for one thing, you wear a ring. And then you say you do nothing. I suppose it is possible that you might be a fabulously rich widow, but in that event you would probably be about to marry our friend David, and, somehow, I can't feel that is the case. If so, you are making as a step-mother a very poor start.'

His eyes creased with soundless laughter, disarming her. She said, 'Of course you are right. I do live entirely on my husband. But you think that is wrong.'

'No, no. I love normal people. The strange thing is, one sees remarkably few of them. You really are devoted to your husband, then? Mend his socks and so on? For better or for worse? For how many years has this been going on?'

'Years and years,' she said lightly. Again she put down her empty glass; again, rapid, courteous, he provided a full one. She turned now and faced the room. It was, although she had not seen more people come in, crowded. David was not there. She said, her lips feeling strangely numb, 'Perhaps I really should go and help him with Annette—'

'You can't make up your mind, can you? The fascination of that horrible child is too great.'

'I feel guilty.'

'Of course.' Like a teacher whose pupil has miraculously given the right answer, he bathed her in approbation, moving nearer as though to pat her in pleasure. 'Of course you do. But why? She isn't your child. Nobody else feels guilty. Why, my dear, should you?'

'I don't know,' she said, then laughed, shaking her head, repeating, 'I don't know.' Standing at the side of the room, pressed into the corner as though in the wings waiting to make an entrance, she felt safe, supported. Her only remaining fear was that he would leave her. For the first time he looked up, away from her, his large, amiable face raised and alert like an old dog catching some fresh, disturbing scent. She began, tumbling over her words, to ask him something. He silenced her with a quick, curt gesture and said, as though struck into a kind of ecstasy, 'Good God, look who's here!'

Peering round him briefly as round some great fortress rock, she saw a girl standing in the doorway, square, motionless, her hands dug deep into the pockets of an old duffle coat. Behind the girl, in an attitude of waiting, passive and unconscious as though he were asleep, was Mark.

CHAPTER 23

THE girl looked quickly round the room. In her trousers and coat she gave the impression of a small, impatient general just arrived from the front line.

'Where's David?'

'My dear, as far as I know he's putting Annette to bed.'

'Still?' She glanced at her watch, thickly strapped. 'At this hour?'

'They weren't even here when we arrived. We had to wait on the stairs.'

'Where's Veronica, then?'

'Not here.' They looked round, reminded that there was something missing, belatedly searching for it. 'Certainly not here. Come to think of it, she never came. There was some other woman.'

'Who?'

'Never seen her before. Maybe she's still here. Maybe she's gone.'

'Annette is ill or something.'

The girl reached back and took Mark's hand, pulling him forward, introducing him. Then quickly, without apology, she went away.

'Haven't I seen you somewhere before?' a man asked, turning from the drink he was pouring as though the quantity of poison depended on Mark's answer.

'I think not.' He pushed his hand over his forehead nervously. 'I'm good on faces.'

'Funny. I could have sworn—' He handed Mark the glass. Looking down into its small, acid depth Mark heard the weird sound of a party approaching full tide: the savage and indefinite roar, the sibilant undertone, the rise and slight shriek and immediate death of individual voices. He felt strongly, keeping his eyes on the glass, that the sound had suddenly become directed into one channel, was flowing towards and encircling him. He drank, but did not look up. 'Putzi . . . Putzi . . . Bobby's dog . . . Didn't you hear about . . .' He looked up then, quickly, but only met the vague and amiable gaze of the man with the two bottles in his hands and the well-arranged, distantly anticipating faces of two women in hats.

'Do you live near here?' they asked. Not a flicker showed that they knew the other had spoken.

'Yes. Yes, quite near.' He darted a look from side to side: strangers. He looked back to the two ladies, piercing and screwing down their flimsy faces against the uneasy backcloth of the day. 'I haven't met you before, have I?'

'I don't think so. Are you in films?'

'No,' he answered, and drank, keeping his eyes on them in the hopeless, irrational conviction that if he did not recognise anyone he himself would remain unrecognised. 'The fog,' he said, 'is very thick.'

'Isn't it? It took us over an hour to get up here from Chelsea.'

'Chelsea?'

'And then to find David not here was so strange. You know we had to wait on the stairs?'

'David?'

They had begun to look at him curiously, tearing their faces away from his fastening eyes. 'David Sangston. This *is* his party, you know. Philip, darling, I am dying to hear about Majorca . . .' They moved together, forcing their way between the two script writers. Mark followed them quickly, bending his head as though to tunnel a way between the faceless, resisting bodies.

Antonia, without thinking, had flattened herself against the bookcase; crouched, hiding, behind the large man. She did not know what to do, any more than she would have known if suddenly she had found herself conscious in somebody else's dream. She had no right to be here: this was private, a time of Mark's which it was unnatural, almost horrible to witness. Her heart leapt and struggled in a sudden wave of sickness. At the same time, as in listening to words spoken in delirium or seeing the slight indication of some buried corpse, she felt a dreadful curiosity, a compulsion to remain, to make certain of what she already knew. She asked, knowing her voice was shaking, 'Who is it?'

'Extraordinary!' He had temporarily forgotten her and now came back to her excited, delighted, his face shining with a sort of bland joy. 'Extraordinary thing!'

'Isn't that the same man?' someone asked, turning slightly towards him.

'Indeed. Mark Painton.'

'What's he doing here?'

'I suppose Barbara brought him. What an extraordinary thing!'

'Please—' Antonia said. She overcame herself, smiled, locking her hands away behind her back. 'Please explain.'

'It's the most remarkable story.' He captured another full glass. She was forced to hold out her hand and take it, tasting its bitterness in one gulp and then standing with her hands behind her again, her head bent, quite still. 'I happen to know this man, so of course to me there is an added interest. A most respectable fellow, a solicitor, a very good practice, an excellent, as they say, type of client. In fact, like yourself, a perfectly normal person. Three or four children, two of whom I happened to meet yesterday in—of all places—Madam Tussaud's.'

He waited for a moment, but she did not smile. Her attitude was that of someone being beaten; passive, dogged, her shoulders rigid. 'He was behaving rather strangely then, but I attributed it to the fact that one of his small girls had been sick on the stairs. Do forgive me if I'm boring you, but the background is important, you understand. He is the type of man who takes his children to Madam Tussaud's on a Saturday afternoon and is faced with them being sick on the stairs. You appreciate that?'

She nodded, one further inclination of her head. 'But what happened,' she asked quietly, 'after that?'

'Mind you, my dear, I'd never met this man socially before this. Met him in Court, of course—I am, by the way, a barrister—and in conference. But I would have said he was, you know, a dull dog.'

'Yes,' she said. 'But what happened?'

'First, I meet him in Madam Tussaud's. Then this morning I am innocently drinking my beer in our local when in he comes with little Barbara. Why is a respectable family man on a Sunday morning far from home with a girl like Barbara? Well, it's none of my business, after all. Barbara is a dear child, I am very fond of her. What she finds in Painton, or where she found him, is beyond me. Never mind, one must in these cases be tolerant. There was a young man there with one of these frightful Kraut dogs. Admittedly frightful, admittedly Kraut, but not, as far as one could tell, doing much harm. Quite suddenly Painton seizes this dog and attempts to murder it. I mean he literally took hold of it'—his hands closed round the invisible dog and then violently rejected it—'and threw it to the ground! Extraordinary! The next thing was that the young man—terribly queer, of course, but I thought remarkably pugnacious—was going at Painton hammer and tongs. Uproar, there was. Complete uproar.'

'And the girl?' Antonia asked. 'Barbara?'

'Oh, I managed to separate them. Poor old Painton

was in a frightful mess—of course, the boy fought like a woman, only interested in drawing blood. Barbara took him away.'

'Who?'

'Painton. It seems his wife has left him. Perhaps that accounts for it. What I can't understand is why she should bring him here. He stood in some danger this morning of being lynched, poor fellow. Would that to you have seemed possible?'

'I don't know,' she said. 'I don't know.' She was cold, shivering with disgust in the vast, glacial wilderness of this nightmare which was not her own, which perhaps had been dreamed without her knowledge for a long time, carried secretly about with him, an escape, a fantasy of freedom more pitiful, more abortive than any reality. Her own dream, in which she had seen herself desired, possessed without love, was forgotten. 'Do you think he is having an affair with this—Barbara? Do you think he is in love with her?' The words were strung on a voice strained to its extreme limit.

'An affair? But, my dear, I imagine so!' The benign smile warmed his whole face, a smile long and shadowless as noon; it sank, as she watched it, incredibly slowly; a full minute went by before it was changed to a face of alarm, doubt, positive concern. He put forward his hand, but she avoided it, ran behind him, escaped him as he made a slow, blundering movement to catch her arm.

CHAPTER 24

BUILDINGS reared up from the fog, lighthouses, rocks, masts. High up in the dense and yellow air one lighted window blinked palely to another. Between these solid towers of brick and glass, each combed with lighted cells, each containing great weights of the living, dying and dead, lagoons and canals of fog deepened, closed over the vague shapes of abandoned cars, became impassable. In Sheldon Road the Paintons' house, unlit, sank without trace; on either side of it the glow from the landlady's basement, the perpetual square of light from the upstairs window shone like beacons marking the place of some forgotten wreck.

Antonia, in the long, thickly carpeted corridor of David's flat, steadied herself and then, seeing the painted walls reeling towards her, abruptly sat down. She sat like someone waiting in a hospital corridor, her back to the wall, her hands grasping the arms of the chair, her head bent. After a moment, which seemed to her an indefinite time, a void, an echo chamber of unidentified humming and fluting sound, she got up and walked on. She had one definite purpose, which was to sit still in the dark and wait: to wait without thinking; to sit in the dark by herself and wait. She knew that if she left the flat she would be helpless. She knew that if she attempted to find her way home she would get lost. She knew that there would be no one to ask, no taxies. She also knew that there was nowhere else she could go. All these things, which normally would have seemed uncertain, arguable, inducing a state of indecision and worry, were now obvious. She directed herself carefully towards the simple objective of an open door at the end of the passage.

'Oh,' someone said. 'She's still here.'

'Who?'

'That woman.'

'You,' a new, a masculine voice said, 'are the man who behaved so venomously to poor Bobby's puppy. What are you doing here?' The crimson face jerked up abruptly between Mark and his glass; he was in the absurd position of embracing, as though tenderly protective, the bulky, tweeded figure. As she had not changed her clothes, the bow tie still spiking aggressively under her chin, he could not pretend even to himself that he did not recognise her.

'I think it is scandalous of you. What are you *doing* here?'

'If I had known,' Mark murmured, smiling as though this were love, 'I shouldn't have come, I assure you. It's as much of a surprise to me—' He tried to move his arm, but it was impossible.

'If you had known what? What surprise? You mean

you weren't invited? What?' She spat hail; her eyes, traced with little broken veins, were militant, full of rheum; there was the smell on her breath of stale whisky and shag. He backed slightly away now holding his glass at arm's length. 'In a manner of speaking,' he said, 'I was invited, yes.'

'I suppose Barbara brought you?'

'Yes.'

'We should have called the police. We shouldn't have allowed you to get off scot-free. My blood boils when I think of it.' She was advancing step by step, trembling a little as though her blood were indeed boiling, agitating her like a kettle.

'Molly's off,' someone said, and there was a little uneasy laughter. Mark realised that a small space had been cleared, that this was some sort of familiar sport in which the woman, red-eyed, was the attacker and he the ignorant and ineffectual victim. If she had been a man he would have stood his ground. As it was, pressing backwards, he felt only disgust, a feeling of complete unreality, as though being insulted in a dream.

'I'm sorry,' he said gravely. 'I hope the dog is well?'

There was an urgent whisper behind him. 'Painton!' Before he could turn round, Teasdown had leant over with a long arm and hauled him away, pulling him out into the corridor and slamming the door behind him.

'My dear Painton,' Teasdown gasped. His face was full of alarm, its customary benevolence agitated,

213

peaked like an anxious hen. 'My dear Painton, you must leave, you really must leave!'

'I didn't know you were here. I didn't see you.'

'Poor Molly is quite uncontrollable. Supposing we go and have a quiet drink?'

'Where?'

'At my club. Yes, we could go to my club.' He looked up and down the corridor desperately. 'You should really not have come, you know. Have you a car?'

'No,' Mark said. 'I can't think she's as dangerous as all that. I can't go.'

'A taxi, then. You think we should get a taxi?'

'I'm sure we shouldn't; it's impossible to drive in this fog. In any case, I can't—'

'You can't stay here, you know. Why not,' he pleaded, 'go home?'

'I don't want to go home!' Mark said irritably. 'Have you seen Barbara?'

'Barbara.' Teasedown put his hand heavily on Mark's arm, as though to support himself. He looked suddenly unwell, like a man who has thought of food on a Channel crossing. 'I do suggest to you, you would be wise to go home. We could perhaps walk?'

'Are you implying, by any chance, that—'

'No, no. I am implying nothing, my dear fellow, nothing.' Teasedown had a sickening vision of a heap of plump and profitable briefs vanishing; of himself selling, with dignity, hats. He was in horrible conflict. He said, 'I really only thought we might both remove ourselves to a more—congenial atmosphere. Such as my club?'

'Yes,' Mark said, 'but I shall be leaving with Barbara.'

Defeated, Teasedown shrugged his shoulders, sighed. 'Dog doesn't eat dog,' he said irrelevantly. He hurried off down the corridor and knocked on the closed door, glancing furtively back as the door of the sitting-room opened and Molly charged, her head lowered, out into the corridor.

Lying on her back, Antonia heard breathing. She moved her hand to the edge of the bed, felt cautiously in the darkness and touched what must be another bed beside the one on which, gratefully, she had fallen. For a moment she did not move. The breathing continued, shallow, irregular. She propped herself up with some difficulty and feeling a table, a lamp, managed to switch it on. A deep pink glow, hardly light, illuminated her own bed, leaving the other in shadow. Annette was curled, making no more than a small swelling under the pink eiderdown; her head somehow unnaturally protruded, though only just, on to a frilled pillow; for a few seconds after the light was switched on she unconsciously and rhythmically sucked her thumb; then again, except for the uncertain breathing, there was silence.

Antonia fell back again on the pillows. Without moving her head she looked round the room. Wherever she looked she saw the bead eyes, pot bellies, contorted grins of Annette's familiars. Here the world of childhood had been made terrifying, obscene, by the elimination of all mystery, eccentricity or pain: wherever the eye searched it fell flatly on sexy rabbits; winged midgets simpered insanely round the walls; suffused by the rosy brothel light, the room was a cosy hell, a child's hell. To Antonia, looking round with slow and fearful eyes, the four walls seemed to heave slightly, the menagerie to move.

She shut her eyes. The breathing, the heaving of the walls continued, like the motion of a ship under a blind man. She opened them again, staring up at the ceiling, trying to fix it still. Then she turned on her stomach, holding the sides of the bed as though it were a surf board, her face buried in the pillow.

'Mrs. Painton?' The whisper was sepulchral, a sighing of ghosts. She did not move, her breath damping the pillow, her body pressed to the bed.

'Mrs Painton.'

She felt a hand on her shoulder. She said, without turning, 'Go away.' There was a long silence, and at last she managed to raise her head, immediately dropping it again when she saw Teasedown's face hanging apparently disembodied like a lantern, open-mouthed with concern. As though with the clicking of the door latch time had reversed and was now slowly winding itself backwards, she felt that the future had run out; what happened now would draw her back along the corridor, through the hostile room, towards the dim mirror and into David's arms; from there an infinite journey, the drawing on the wall, the hot chintz bedroom, the attic, the lane, the hopeless and distant figure of Mark in a forgotten bedroom. All this, unless she could stop it, was about to begin again.

'Mrs Painton—'

She pushed herself off the bed, stood upright.

'I must deeply apologise,' Teasedown whispered. 'I must—'

She brushed past him, groping towards the door.

'I shouldn't—' Teasedown wailed quietly. 'My dear girl, don't— Where are you going?'

She flung open the door. Mark, slowly, carefully running, his arms and mouth stretched wide, seemed to sink down a long, softly lit well towards her.

CHAPTER 25

THE moment of waking, however physically abrupt, is slow, confused; the dream is not over; the body stiffens, becomes weighted with consciousness but still longs to fly, to escape down endless paths; lust, terror, longing move like wisps of smoke behind a closed window.

Mark stopped running, as though suddenly, in the moment of raising his foot and embracing the air, petrified. At the other end of the corridor a group of people were shouting, clustered tightly round a squat brown figure, who seemed to gesticulate desperately, without sound. Behind Antonia, Teasedown stood like a mournful statue of some elder statesman, his hands locked, one knee bent, his head inclined as though never again to look the world in the face. Antonia stood quite still.

'Hullo.'

'Hullo, Mark.'

'What are you doing here?'

She did not answer. Incredulously, he came nearer. 'Where have you been? What's happened? Why are you here?'

'Where's David?'

218

'How should I know? I've been damned nearly torn to pieces by that bitch. She ought to be locked up.'

'Your tie is crooked.' She looked past him. They were hustling the woman away, coaxing her out of the door. Their voices grew fainter as they persuaded her down into the fog. The flat was silent.

'Did Teasedown know you were here?' Mark asked.

The woman Antonia had first met came wandering out of the sitting-room, followed by one of the script writers. She came down the corridor muffling herself, making little shudders and gestures of cold and disapproval. 'Oh,' she said, looking at Antonia, 'so you're still here. Have you seen David?'

'No,' Antonia said.

'I do think it's most strange. Where is the child?'

'Asleep.'

'Then I think, Philip darling, we should go. There seems nothing to stay for.'

They went, like leaves blown by a gentle wind. A man and a woman came out of the sitting-room. The man called, 'Anybody seen Barbara?'

Mark, Antonia and Teasedown said nothing. The man called amiably, 'You—didn't you come with Barbara?'

Mark was silent. Antonia said, 'He is talking to you.' Mark said, 'No. No, I haven't seen her.'

'I was going to offer her a lift. Never mind. Can't be helped. Good night.' They went, closing the door behind them. To Mark, Antonia and Teasedown at the same time came the thought that they were now alone.

'It's ridiculous,' Mark said. 'They are here somewhere.' He made a slight, a tentative bluster in the silence. Raising his voice, he called, 'Sangston?'

'Be quiet. You'll wake the child.'

'What child?'

'Annette. She wouldn't have gone without telling you, would she?'

'Who?'

'The girl. What is her name—Barbara?'

Their voices, hushed in the empty corridor, made little sound, were as distant as voices heard on waking. They did not address questions to each other, but to themselves; no question was answered or ever would be; the sound passed from one to the other and became, with little difference, silence.

'Well, we can't just stand about here. Why don't we look for them?'

'Look for them,' Antonia said.

'I do think—' Teasedown began. They had forgotten him. He blundered forward to offer his thought, his hands extended as though to drive them both away. Annette, in a pink nightdress, clasping the pink rabbit, stepped quietly into his place. She addressed herself to Antonia with a kind of implacable malice. 'You could all go home,' she said, 'if it didn't mean leaving me alone.'

'Alone?'

'Where are they?'

220

'Who?'

'Your father and—'

'Barbara.'

'Oh, they went ages ago.'

'Went?'

'To the pub.'

'Which pub?'

'I expect the one over the road. They're getting married.'

'Come, Annette, back to bed. You're still dreaming.'

'I shall be a bridesmaid, they said. And wear pink.'

'What are you talking about?'

'Who are you? Aren't you Charlotte's father?'

'Who are you talking about?'

'It is perfectly clear. The child is simply, I mean, telling us that her father is going to be married.'

'That's right. That's what they said in the bath-room.'

'But they can't just decide like that, so suddenly—'

'I think it was not so sudden.'

'Oh no, they've been talking about it for ages. You know, how do you like Barbara and all that. Have they all gone?'

'I must go.'

'Well, you can't all go and leave me alone. I get frightened.'

'Wait for me, Mark. Wait for me.'

'Then you will have to stay, Mr Teasedown. I think I would like you to read me a story. You can read to me and Cuddlepie, because Cuddlepie has never heard the nice stories that Annette knows, has he, darling? And Cuddlepie is glad that Annette is going to have a nice Mummy to bath her and put her to bed and not have to go to that nasty old Auntie Veronica any more. . . . Mr Teasedown! Are you coming?'

Back down the stairs, running past the wilting hydrangeas, the closed doors, time streaming backwards. She ran, stumbling, jumping the stairs, and came no nearer to Mark. He hesitated for a moment in front of the great wave of fog and then was gone. She plunged after him, striking out with her hands, choking, calling, 'Mark!' Her foot struck the kerb and she fell. Looking up, feeling herself drowning, she saw a wavering and indistinct light and Mark, no clearer than a shadow, seen and immediately gone. She got up and, holding out her hands, pushed: the door swung back, and she was momentarily dazzled by the brass and glass, the deafening brilliance of the small room.

'Are they here?'

He didn't answer, but began pushing his way through to the end of the bar. She followed him, frightened for him and for herself, but knowing that she was powerless to stop him. David and the girl were sitting on a bench by the gas fire. He was leaning forward, holding her hand in both of his. She was looking fondly at her up-ended feet and smiling. She did not stop smiling when Mark stood over them.

'Hullo, Mark. Do you know David? I'm afraid we ran out on you.'

'Of course,' David said, moving reluctantly. 'And Antonia. How clever of you to find us here.'

'We thought we'd escaped,' the girl said.

'Won't you both sit down?'

'Because you know,' the girl smiled at Antonia, 'I am petrified and really need so much advice. You live so near. You must come—is this right?—to tea and bring some of your children. I say, won't it be wonderful when we have tea?' She giggled shortly, glancing at Mark her first look of coquetry, of evasion. He turned, having said nothing, and started to push his way back through the crowd. Antonia, looking back, saw them moving together again, the interruption already forgotten.

They walked at a slight distance from each other, the man first, the woman following, their footsteps the only sound in a deserted world. They walked along Sheldon Road, in and out of the pale haze of lamplight, in the same peculiar formation, disassociated and yet undeniably together, like strangers returning to the same boarding-house or lovers in elaborate disguise. He opened a gate and could be heard falling over something in the dark garden.

'Blast this damned pram. Why can't they put it away?'

'I'll put it away tomorrow.'

There was the slight jangle of keys, the scraping of a lock. The woman turned on a light, and for a moment after they moved together there was one

223

shape against the brightness, looking inward. A black shadow darted between their feet, swift and black as a rat, unnoticed. Then the door slammed shut, the sound of it in the dense silence loud and in some way curiously final.